One of his hands still cupped her face, and he leaned his head near hers.

"Safire, this has been the best part of the whole evening to me—right here, finding out something real about you. You are beautiful. Don't let that change. Don't squander it away. Don't play it away. It's...amazing."

Safire didn't realize she was holding her breath until she opened her mouth to say something. But she didn't know what to say. The intense look on this man's face—so near to hers—took her breath away. His concern over her feelings moved something inside her. His earnest gaze froze her to the spot. His deep voice sent tingles through her.

She nodded once and smiled weakly, not knowing what to say. They seemed so different that she didn't really expect to see him again, not for another date. Things had gotten a bit tense between them at the sports bar. In the end, he was just a little too conservative for her taste.

She turned to get in her car, and he turned toward his. Safire had turned her key in the lock and opened the door before she felt his hand on her back. She turned around to find him immediately in front of her, taking her in his arms. When Darien kissed her, those soft, kissable lips felt like warm, melted chocolate. Her lips parted at their gentle, platonic touch.

But their kiss didn't remain chaste.

Books by Yasmin Sullivan

Harlequin Kimani Romance

Return to Love
Love on the High Seas
Captivated Love

YASMIN SULLIVAN

grew up in upstate New York and St. Thomas, Virgin Islands, from which her family hails. She moved to Washington, D.C., to attend college and has earned degrees from Howard University and Yale University. As an academic writer, she has published on works by Frederick Douglass, Harriet Jacobs, James Baldwin, Maya Angelou and Ed Bullins, as well as the writing of the Negritude Movement and historical fiction treating emancipation in the Danish West Indies/United States Virgin Islands. She currently lives in Washington, D.C., where she teaches with a focus on African-American and Caribbean literatures. When she is not teaching, she also does creative writing and works on mosaics.

CAPTIVATED
Love

YASMIN SULLIVAN

HARLEQUIN® KIMANI™ ROMANCE

For my mother, father, brother and grandmother,
who have given me the richness of the human heart;
for Jennie and Tanya, who have been my sister-friends;
for Madeline, Freddie and William,
who have shaped my vision of love;
for Vionette and Lois,
who have inspired the romantic in me;
and for Jimmie, who was somebody to dream with.

Recycling programs
for this product may
not exist in your area.

ISBN-13: 978-0-373-86368-6

CAPTIVATED LOVE

Copyright © 2014 by Yasmin Y. DeGout

For questions and comments about the quality of this book please contact us at CustomerService@Harlequin.com.

HARLEQUIN®
www.Harlequin.com

Printed in U.S.A.

Dear Reader,

I think that the people we love and those who love us help us to know ourselves, and our interactions with them help us evolve as human beings. They can be our shelter in times of hurt and our inspiration to create great things. They can shield us from bitterness, and they can help us love the spark within ourselves. This is true of friends and family, but especially of lovers.

I hope that this novel reveals the way we grow through our interplay with those we love. This is what Safire Lewis and Darien James have to find out along their journey together—whether they can evolve with each other, whether they can inspire each other. I'm so grateful that you've chosen to share their voyage with me.

I would love to hear your impressions of this book. Please write me at yasminhu@aol.com.

Warm wishes,

Yasmin

Chapter 1

Safire Lewis shifted in her swivel chair, turning from the computer to the open books on the long table in the law library. She loved her work, but a paralegal wasn't what she had set out to become. It was supposed to be a learning interlude on the way to law school. Her parents were gone by then, so she knew she would have to make it independently, and this seemed a way to do that. Now she was ready to make a change, and she already had plans set in motion.

She would have to fight to do it on her own, but it had been that way for a long time. After she lost her parents, she became determined to make it on her own terms—fiercely determined. She was used to fighting, and she was used to going after what she wanted. It was how she had come this far and how she would go on to get what she really wanted—once she finally decided what that was.

Safire tagged a page in one of the books, picked up the phone and dialed her sister's cell phone number.

"Hey, sis. Are we still on for this Saturday?" Her sister rattled off a list of stops they would be making to look for her wedding dress. "I'll be there," Safire said. "And I'll be there to watch Philly tomorrow night….Give your hunky fiancé all my love….Okay, Angelina. See you tomorrow."

Safire hung up the phone, stretched and began rubbing the back of her neck with both hands. She wanted a vacation. She'd missed hers earlier that year when one of her bosses went into labor. She'd had to cancel her plans for a singles cruise. She didn't mind because her sister got to go, and her sister needed it more than she did. But she had wanted that time to do some thinking and to relieve some of her tension, and what better way to relieve tension than to find a sexy single? Yes, she was used to going after what she wanted. Safire shook her head to get rid of her salacious thoughts and turned back to her work.

When she heard the door open, she had her nose in one of the law books on the table and thought it was one of the student interns they had taken on over the summer. The interns were supposed to lighten the load, but until they learned what they were doing, they were more a nuisance than a help.

When she looked up, however, she found not one of the interns but a well-dressed gentleman looking tentatively her way. And he was gorgeous. Safire couldn't help but smile.

He had skin just darker than milk chocolate—sweet enough to lick until it melted in your mouth—and his large brown eyes were astute and attentive. His lips were kissably thick, set in an angular jaw that led to high, chiseled cheekbones. He wore his hair in long braids that were pulled back into a bundle and anchored at the nape of his neck.

Safire shifted her chair so that she could see beyond the table and continued her open perusal.

He was wearing an athletic-cut navy suit that flared at his broad shoulders and tapered just a bit at his waist. She could sense the muscles of his arms beneath the sleeves, and his contoured thighs struggled for release from the pant legs. Her eyes lingered over his center on the way back up. It protruded just enough to hint at the dense manhood that lay beneath. Safire almost licked her lips.

The suit was set off with a white shirt and a cobalt tie, and he carried a black leather satchel. He looked like a young attorney, which pleased Safire greatly. The firm needed some color higher up.

"Excuse me, I—" he said, his voice a rich bass that sent tingles through Safire's body.

Safire cut him off. "You've *got* to be looking for me," she said, getting up from her chair and shrugging off her blazer.

Safire wore a purple miniskirt that matched her blazer, as well as a lavender chiffon camisole and her black two-and-a-half-inch pumps. This was her usual work attire, and she liked it because it showed off her legs and could transition into the evening if she went out.

"Pardon?" he said.

"You've *got* to be looking for me," she repeated, positioning her rear on the tabletop and crossing her legs in front of her. "I've been looking for you, too."

Safire was always bold, partly in fun, partly in all seriousness. She could tell that her handsome stranger wasn't used to this at all, and his hesitation only enticed Safire all the more—that and something sweet in his eyes.

"Uh, are you Janice Wilson? I just left Mr. Benson, and he said that I could stop in to introduce myself to you. You deal with copyrighting?"

"Aw," Safire said and then gave a little pout. "You're looking for Janice."

"I'm afraid I am."

"Well, you're too gorgeous to give away. What about after that?"

"After that?" He seemed a bit puzzled.

"Yes, are you done for the day after you speak with Janice?" Safire scooted off the table and put her hand out as she approached the man. "I'm Safire Lewis. Pleased to meet you."

"Hello. I'm Darien James."

Now that she was standing next to him, she could gauge his height. He must be about six feet because she was five feet eight inches, and he had a couple of inches on her even in her heels. She looked up at him and smiled.

"If you're free after you see Janice, let's go to happy hour. I'll be done in an hour, and it's nearby."

"Uh, I'm not sure how long I'll be with Ms. Wilson. Perhaps a rain check."

"Rain check nothing, Mr. James. You're not getting away, hottie that you are."

Safire took his arm as if they were out on a stroll and led him back into the hall.

"If you're already tied up, now's the time to say so. If not, we're on."

Down the hall, Safire tapped on Janice's office door and poked her head in. She hadn't let go of Mr. James's arm and ushered him in when Janice nodded.

"Ms. Wilson, this is Darien James, my date for happy hour this evening. We need him done within the hour because happy hour at Jake's ends at seven. And don't go getting any ideas of your own."

Janice laughed and got up from her desk, holding her hand out to Darien. Her blue suit with its calf-length skirt and billowy jacket looked matronly next to Safire's purple mini. Safire was kidding about Janice getting ideas. Janice was long married with two school-age children and rarely went out after work. Safire liked to give Janice a chuckle every now and again. Her coworkers knew her sense of humor and relied on it to lighten their long days.

"Good afternoon, Mr. James. Mr. Benson buzzed a few minutes ago to say that you would be stopping in. I was wondering whether you'd gotten lost."

"He was in perfectly good hands," Safire said.

"I see that he was. Come have a seat."

Safire turned to leave. "I'll be in the lobby in an hour," she said to Janice. "Don't let him keep me waiting."

Back in her office, Safire began wrapping up her research for Mr. Hines. It was a criminal case under state jurisdiction involving the mistreatment of a minor, and since cases involving children were Safire's specific interest, she tore through the research. She had already traced the applicable law and had the relevant statutory leads. She had collected all the on-point court decisions she could find, and now she only had to check the relevant cases to see if any of the decisions had been reversed, overruled or criticized.

This kind of suit was why she wanted to become a lawyer or work with children. She wanted to make a difference, not only through research but by having her own cases. Maybe it was because she knew what it was like to be young and feel vulnerable and alone. She was still in high school when her mother died. Then her father went. With her older sister taking care of their younger brother, she knew she had to look out for herself. And she hated feeling vulnerable. She'd made up her mind to rid herself of that feeling and pursue whatever she would have pursued had the foundation not been pulled from under her feet. She wanted to give that to other young people—that determination, that empowerment, that fierceness.

Safire worked for half an hour more and then started packing up the books she had used, keeping out the ones in which she'd tagged pages. She collected her notes, shut down the computer and looked at her watch.

While she was working, her mind stayed focused on the task, but now Safire's thoughts ran back to the ever-so-sexy Mr. Darien James. It was time to get to the lobby, or she might miss him. She grabbed her blazer, collected her purse from her office and said her usual goodbyes. She popped into the restroom to spruce up, taking the clip out of her hair to let the long curls fall down and refreshing her makeup. Then she stopped at the receptionist's desk.

"Is Darien James still in Janice's office?" she asked.

"Yes, he is," the receptionist said.

"Good. I'll be waiting for him in the lobby. Have a good night."

Safire waved and stepped onto the elevator. In the lobby, her heels ticked over the marble floor as she made her way to the central fountain, nodding to the guard on her way. She loved the click of heels and was rarely without them. It made her feel as if she was going somewhere, as if she had a presence. She took a quarter out of her purse and tossed it into the fountain, hoping that Darien James would turn out to be all that she thought he would be.

And what was that? Safire wasn't sure, but he was handsome and sweet—a dangerous and formidable combination and one that was rare in Safire's world. She hadn't really noticed that before. She went out a lot and dated a lot. It was part of her determination to embrace life, part of the willpower that kept her from being undone by the loss of her parents. She pursued men the way she pursued everything else—fiercely. But unlike an education or a career, men could also be a distraction from what was really important, what was really worth pursuing. Safire was keeping her eyes on what counted and never took men too seriously. The lookers she dated were generally a bit full of themselves, basically because they were lookers. It was easy to catch them, have fun with them and then throw them back into the sea for some less focused fisher.

Darien James hadn't seemed that way at all. He seemed down-to-earth and unpretentious, a fact that made him all the more irresistible. In fact, it made him seem a little dangerous. Maybe he was different, different enough to fall for. Safire shrugged at the thought, which was unlike her. If nothing else, he was fine—capital F-I-N-E. Hopefully, he knew how to use his God-given talents. She sure as hell wanted to find out.

There was no telling how long he might be, so Safire sat on the retaining wall that skirted the fountain and took her phone out of her purse to call one of her girlfriends and talk about her latest dish—the one she wanted to be her dish, anyway. Camilla picked up on the second ring.

"Hey, girl," Safire said. "I might not have long, but I have a date for happy hour tonight. He's as good-looking as all get-out and seems sweet on top of that, not full of himself like the usual hottie….You may get to meet him. I have to meet him first for myself—really meet him. I'll let you know how it turns out and whether he tastes as good as he looks."

Safire moved the phone from her ear as Camilla squealed. She glanced up, however, and there was Darien James getting off the elevator. She moved the phone back to her ear.

"Here he is, girl. I gotta go."

She clicked the phone shut, put it back in her bag and got up to make her way toward Darien.

As she neared him, he slowed and blinked twice.

"I hope you're not surprised to see me," Safire said.

"Well, yes. I didn't think you were serious. And your hair is different."

"Serious as an accident on I-95. You going?"

"Uh…" He seemed to think about it a moment.

Safire watched him closely in those few seconds. She saw the shift in his face as his reluctance began to drain away, and then he turned and looked into her face, clearly intrigued by the woman standing in front of him. Finally, he gave her a little smile.

"Yes. Happy hour. Why not?"

"Good. We get to really meet. Are you open to that?"

"Sure," he said. "I just hadn't planned on going out tonight. But you've convinced me. I'd like to get to know you better, and a few hours in the company of a beautiful woman can soothe a work-worn spirit." He held out his arm to her. "Let's go."

Safire took the arm Darien offered, and the two mini-stepped through the revolving door together. They came out on the other side laughing, and Safire directed them down the street to Jake's.

Jake's was a sports bar on the corner, and it was always packed with downtown types at happy hour. It had huge television screens and a large bar in the center of the room. Booths were stationed along the walls, but these were filled by now. High tables with tall stools occupied the rest of the space. Safire and Darien took seats at one of these, and Safire signaled a waiter.

"Can I get you drinks?"

"Make mine a virgin strawberry daiquiri," Safire said, rolling her neck, "or I might end up on the floor."

"Make mine the same," Darien said.

His voice was smooth and resonant, and Safire loved the thrill it sent up her spine.

"You don't have to forgo the alcohol because of me," Safire said. "Go ahead. Unwind."

"I don't really drink."

That was a little odd to Safire, but she didn't mind. Cute as he was, he really did seem to be rather unassuming, as well. Safire liked that.

"Why not?"

"I don't know. I guess I wasn't raised around alcohol. And I have a very hectic schedule, so I don't actually get out much." He shrugged.

"I shouldn't have a virgin daiquiri myself. It must be four hundred calories even without the alcohol," Safire complained. "But in for a penny, in for a pound—in this case an American pound." She chuckled. "What do you want to eat?" she asked, turning to the menu. "We can order real food if you're hungry. I'm fine with wings."

"I'm— I actually don't eat meat."

Aw. Worrisome as it was—she'd never gone out with a vegetarian or vegan—Safire was glad to be sitting across from someone with convictions. This one wasn't all play. That could be a good thing.

"Oh, they must have other stuff on the menu. If not, we can go somewhere else."

"I'll have some potato skins," he said and closed the menu. "I'll be fine."

In the momentary silence that followed, Darien smiled at her, and his smile opened up his whole face, letting her peek at the boy she hadn't known and the inside of the man he was now. She loved that smile.

"So how long have you worked for the Law Offices of Benson and Hines?" he asked.

"I've been with them almost two years now. Good pay. Interesting work."

"Are you an attorney? You seem kind of young…"

"No, I'm a paralegal, and I'm twenty-three. I couldn't have finished law school already unless I was a child genius."

Safire laughed, and Darien joined her.

"What about you? Will you be joining the firm?"

Darien laughed at that. "No, no. I'm twenty-six, but I'm not a lawyer."

Safire pursed her lips into a pout.

"What is it?" he asked. "Did I say the wrong thing?"

"No, I was just hoping for a brother or sister in the upper ranks. We need some color up in there, if you know what I mean."

Darien chuckled, but then he nodded in understanding.

"I'm sorry that I don't fit the bill. I hope you don't mind having us as a client, though."

His apology was so sincere that it touched Safire. He was a sweetie.

"Who's us?" she asked.

"I work at the Heritage Community Arts, Education and Resource Center of Miami. Benson and Hines has agreed to start doing some pro bono work for our needy, and I'm helping to handle some of the arrangements."

"Why did you need Janice?"

"That was a personal aside. I needed some advice about copyrighting my art. I'm an artist—primarily wood but also metal and clay."

Their drinks and food arrived, and the two began nibbling.

"I'm also a full-time MFA student at Florida International University," Darien said, "but I've worked at the Heritage Center forever. I do some administrative work and teach art."

"Why do you do it?"

"I love it. I love the kids. I love the Heritage Center. I want it to do well."

"I like your fervor."

The passion in Darien's voice drew Safire to him. She slipped off one of her shoes and found his shin with her toes, letting him know how attracted she was.

He paused over his potato skins and looked at her. "You move rather fast, don't you?"

"Is that a bad thing? I go after what I want, and I like to have a good time."

"Does it ever get serious for you?"

"What does that mean? Because I go after what I want, I can't be serious?"

"You can be, but are you?"

"If it gets serious, that's fine. If it doesn't, it wasn't meant to be. I'm serious right now about wanting you."

Safire reached over and touched Darien's face with her sticky fingers. Then she leaned over and kissed the sticky spot, licking the sauce from his face.

Darien let out a heavy breath.

"You do move fast, maybe too fast."

"Doesn't Darien like to come out and play?" Safire teased.

"In my wilder days—in a hot second. Now I take it a bit slower."

Little warning bells had been going off in Safire's head since they started their evening. She liked to play, and Darien seemed a little conservative for her. He didn't drink. He didn't get out much. He didn't eat meat. Now he was into taking it slowly. For the fourth time that evening, Safire wanted to raise her eyebrows. This time she did, giving Darien a genuinely quizzical look. He chuckled.

"I guess I've mellowed."

"But you're not old. What made you a nondrinking, non-partying, veggie-burger-eating stick-in-the-mud?"

"Hold up. I said that I don't drink often. That's not a bad thing. And let's talk about meat."

"No, let's not," Safire said. "Let's get to the real issue—"

"Which is what?" Darien asked.

"A beautiful woman finds you attractive and wants to get to know you."

"That's not a problem. In fact, that's great."

"Then why the brakes?"

Darien leaned back and looked at her. "No one ever tells you no, do they? But then, you're a beautiful woman. Why should they?"

His compliment made Safire smile, despite the tension between them.

"Actually," she said, "you probably don't hear no a lot either. You're a hottie if ever I saw one."

Darien looked down and grinned, but it was clear he was trying not to.

"Thank you, Safire."

"I guess I don't hear no a lot," Safire said, "because I usually look for people I have something in common with."

"I take it that's not me."

Something had softened between them, renewing Safire's desire to know this man. "The verdict is still out on that. How about if we go dancing?"

Darien rolled his eyes, and both of them laughed.

"I guess you're not a big dancer," Safire said.

"I've danced a bit, but not recently. Tell me, what else do you like?"

"I like broad shoulders, like yours." She eyed him tellingly, but he waved her on to the next item. "I like music. I like jazz clubs."

Darien started nodding, and his eyes lit up. "I have an idea. There's a café called Sylvester's about fifteen minutes from here. They have desserts and wine, as well. Sometimes they have poetry readings and live music. I think that tonight they have a jazz band. Let's go check it out."

"Okay."

"Can you follow me in your car?" Darien asked, getting up and taking Safire's arm to steady her.

"Sure."

"I won't be able to stay long, but it should be good."

Safire shook her head. "Is it getting past your bedtime already?" she said, and chuckled.

"You really do think I'm a stick-in-the-mud, don't you?"

"I was just teasing."

"I'm actually a huge night owl, but I still have work to do tonight."

"Then I won't keep you out late."

They smiled at one another, arm hooked in arm, and Darien walked Safire to her car. Then he got his, met her and led them to Sylvester's.

It was a Friday night, so there was a crowd. As they expected, there was a jazz band—a combo of four—filling the stage beyond the café tables. The place was small, and the band was using microphones, so it was much louder than it needed to be. They enjoyed the music, but they couldn't hold a conversation over the sound.

Safire and Darien found a table at the counter along the wall, and Darien got them desserts and smoothies. Darien put his hand on the back of Safire's raised chair. They sat close together and bounced their heads in unison as the band played standards like "A Night in Tunisia," "'Round Midnight," "Night and Day," "Summertime," "Blue Bossa," "God Bless the Child" and "Take the 'A' Train." Safire wished they could dance, but the café was packed, with tables almost touching.

"Do you like the band?" Darien asked, shouting over the music.

Safire nodded without losing the beat.

By the time the set was over, their desserts were gone.

"I hope you liked that," Darien said. "It might be the only thing we have in common."

Safire laughed. "I loved it. If only we could have danced."

"I'm glad you enjoyed it," Darien said.

There was sincerity in his expression and a rather boyish grin on his face at having pleased her. His deep voice crawled down Safire's spine like a caterpillar.

"I did."

"Well, at least there's one thing this nondrinking, nonpartying, veggie-burger-eating—"

Safire started to laugh.

"I'm sorry to turn into a pumpkin before midnight, but I have to get home. Thank you for getting me out of the house for a bit—unexpectedly."

"Anytime," Safire said. "You just let me know. Because I have a life. I like to get out."

"I see why," Darien said as he got down from his stool. Once Safire was standing, he placed his hand on her back. "Let me walk you to your car."

Safire nodded and smiled.

"So how did you come to like jazz?" Darien asked as they neared her car.

It was a question that took Safire off guard and made her think back. "My father," she said. "He would play jazz albums almost every weekend."

Safire recalled waking up on weekends to the sound of her father's jazz records. The sun would be up already, but she would snuggle under the covers listening to the music that filled the house. She knew that her father was in the living room in his easy chair nodding his head in time to the rhythm and that her mother was in the kitchen humming along as she made breakfast. Safire could smell the bacon or sausage as it wafted through the house, and she knew she had to get up, but not right away, not while everything felt so peaceful and the world seemed so bright.

Without warning, tears began to well up in Safire's eyes. Darien had evidently noticed. He stepped toward her and took her face in his palm. He seemed to be waiting for her to say more. Safire didn't know what to say. She wanted those days back so much—those peaceful mornings when everyone was there and everyone was all right. She shook her head to clear it. Then, as if by way of explanation for her sudden fit of sniveling, she began recounting facts of her life that she generally kept hidden.

"He played them almost every weekend until my mother died. I was seventeen, still in high school. Then he stopped playing them. He died two years later."

Darien's other hand came up to Safire's face, and he used his thumbs to wipe away the tears that had fallen.

The pressure of Darien's fingers brought Safire back to the moment. His fingers were gentle, and his caress was filled with caring and understanding. She looked into his face and saw his concern for her, and a sweet ache filled her heart. Then she imagined what she must look like, standing there blubbering.

"You'll have to excuse me. I don't know what has me talking about all of this or—"

"It's okay," Darien said, and his deep timbre sent a shiver up Safire's spine. "I'm so sorry to hear about your parents. You've been on your own for a while."

"Not entirely," she said. "I have siblings and friends. But I had to grow up and become independent quickly. I do all right."

"It explains why you're so mature at such a young age. Maybe it explains even more."

He didn't say what, and Safire wasn't sure if she should ask. She was still wondering what had gotten into her— why these feelings had risen to the top, why now when they never did. She shook it off, regained her composure and looked at Darien.

"Well, Mr. Darien James—nondrinking, non-going-out, veggie-eating, take-it-slow hottie. I guess I better let you go."

One of his hands still cupped her face, and he leaned his head near hers.

"Safire, this has been the best part of the whole evening to me—right here, finding out something real about you. You are beautiful. Don't let that change. Don't squander it away. Don't play it away. It's…amazing."

Safire didn't realize she was holding her breath until she opened her mouth to say something. But she didn't know what to say. The intense look on this man's face— so near to hers—took her breath away. His concern over her feelings moved something inside her, and his earnest gaze froze her to the spot. When she heard his deep voice, tingles went through her.

She nodded once and smiled weakly, not knowing what to say. They seemed so different that she didn't really expect to see him again, not for another date. Things had gotten a bit tense between them at the sports bar. In the end, he was just a little too conservative for her taste.

She went to her car, and he turned toward his. Safire had put her key in the lock and opened the door before she felt his hand on her back. She turned around to find him immediately in front of her, taking her in his arms. When Darien kissed her, those soft, kissable lips felt like warm, melted chocolate. Her lips parted at their gentle, platonic touch.

But their kiss didn't remain chaste. Darien's tongue moved in between Safire's parted lips, and her arms moved to his neck, pulling her closer to his body. His hands slipped farther around her back, feeding a fire that was growing inside her loins.

He stopped as suddenly as he started and stepped back from her.

"Good night, Safire. And thank you again."

With the feelings that had built up inside her, Safire couldn't resist. She smiled her Safire smile and offered, "Are you sure you don't want to come home with me and play?" She knew as she said it that she had broken their reverie.

Darien tipped his head down and leaned in so that his mouth almost touched her ear. "Slow down."

His words in her ear sent a quiver through her frame, but they also shattered the last bit of their mutual trance. She swatted him playfully with her purse.

"You may not be a stick-in-the-mud, but you're certainly too orthodox for me."

"I take it that the jury is now in."

Safire smiled and got into her car. She pulled up beside Darien as he got to his car, waved once as he closed the door and sped off into the night.

Chapter 2

Darien James was more on the casual side. He owned a few suits, but more often than not, he wore jeans with some kind of printed shirt or T-shirt, and to dress that up, he wore a nice shirt or a dashiki or a vest—maybe a jacket, if it was necessary. This was the second time in as many weeks that he'd had to step up his game, and he was starting to like it. He could see how to move back and forth between business and casual without losing sight of what drove him.

The last time had been just over a week ago, when he'd gone to the Law Offices of Benson and Hincs. That was also the day he'd met Safire Lewis and gone out with her. She had a list for him—nondrinking, nonpartying, veggie-burger-eating stick-in-the-mud, or something to that effect. He had a list for her as well, and it included the word *siren.* He hadn't seen her since that night, and they hadn't exchanged personal information, so he didn't think he'd see her again. They seemed to be on different paths or in different places in their lives. She was on the fast track, and he'd gotten off the fast track some time ago—a move for the better, actually.

Now he sat in a conference room at the Nova Investment Firm, where he was representing the Heritage Community Arts, Education and Resource Center of Miami and waiting for the arrival of two more potential corporate backers for some of their programs. Nova had put this together pro bono to help the Heritage Center garner support from the local business community. His role was to describe the programs—the ones being offered already and the ones being added to better serve the community. He had worked at the Heritage Center for so long that he was confident in his ability to do this with minimal preparation. Nonetheless, he'd put together a very professional-looking packet of information.

The backing would also help with their Legal Assistance Program, but he didn't expect Mr. Benson to show up, and he didn't think that anyone from Benson and Hines would be there. He was surprised to see Safire Lewis enter the waiting area and look toward the conference room. It turned out that she was representing the Law Offices of Benson and Hines.

He could see her through the windows surrounding the conference room. Her crescent eyes sparkled with some inner mirth, and her high cheekbones were shaped into plump circles that puckered with her smile. Her lips were thick and full, making Darien remember how soft they were when he kissed her. She had a small, impish nose and a wide forehead. Though her face looked young, innuendo was written subtly over her features—in the way one side of her lips turned up in a smile, and the way she looked at him as if on the sly, as she did now through the window.

Her long hair was piled up on her head, placing an emphasis on her face that made her look young. Well, it made her look twenty-three. But she also flashed that cryptic Safire smile, the one that seemed sweet but that hid the temptress underneath, the one that made her look as if she was having a naughty thought. That was part of her attitude, an air she carried with her—an air of availability. But it wasn't ordinary, not the way she wore it. She carried herself as if she was in control, as if she would be deciding what, how, when…and who. There was an air of loftiness to her that made her untouchable and kept her from seeming coarse or crass or vulgar.

She clacked into the room on two-and-a-half-inch heels wearing a green brocade miniskirt with a matching blazer and a green camisole. It was much like the outfit she'd worn when they'd met. But she was stunning even without the heels and short shirt. These made her attractive in an in-your-face kind of way that Darien found unnecessary. It wasn't his bag, really, or at least it wasn't until he saw it on Safire. She seemed to wear the culture of allure so naturally that it almost disappeared on her, leaving only her long legs and sharp eyes and shapely figure.

Still, she wore it, almost flaunting her beauty. He was used to the types who did this—or tried to do it. They were generally so impressed with themselves that they didn't have time to be impressed with you, and they seemed to know that they could have anyone, so they eventually found someone they thought was better than you. In Darien's experience, the beautiful ones who knew that they were beautiful were a danger, and almost everything he knew about Safire Lewis told him that she was one of these. Everything but the sudden tears that had fallen from her eyes like a brief burst of summer rain.

She was carrying a leather portfolio, which she plopped onto the table in the conference room before rounding to his side. She bent down and whispered, "Hello again, hottie." She gave him a wink that the others could not see, and then she straightened herself, shaking his hand formally before proceeding around the table to introduce herself.

Darien couldn't help being amused by Safire's private greeting. He smiled and played along with her pretense of a polite exchange. He also took this as a signal to begin and pulled the packages he'd prepared out of his briefcase, handing them around the table as he followed Safire's path introducing himself.

"You might want to glance through this as we wait," he said to the potential backers. "The right-hand side has a detailed summary of our programs. Each description identifies our community's need, our achievement goals, our assessment instruments and our projected program budgets, and each one indicates how long the program has been running or whether it's a new addition to our fall lineup. The left-hand side is a packet of the brochures that we have describing the Heritage Center and its programs—current and forthcoming." Darien finished handing out the packets and sat down. "I'll talk about these once everyone is here, but you can browse through them now."

"This is all very professionally done," one of the panel members said.

"Well, we've been running for over fifty years, and we want to keep running for fifty more." That drew genial laughter from the group. "Our programs have brought up SAT scores of participating high school students, and they've actually had an impact on student high school completion rates."

"You seem a lot like the YMCA," another panel member said.

"In some ways we are, but not all. We don't run athletic programs. We do tutoring, family counseling and computer training, and we teach classes in art, reading and writing, music, history, math, science enrichment—"

"I see you've already started." Alberta Evans, the manager of the project for the Nova Investment Firm, came in leading the two potential backers they were waiting for. Darien nodded and handed them all packets. Now they were really ready to begin.

Mrs. Evans opened up the meeting with remarks about their purpose for being there. Then she handed the proceedings over to Darien, who walked them through the packet and the programs. "The last thing I want to point out to you is the brochure for our upcoming fund-raiser. You'll see all the ways you can participate on the back. These programs work, so they're worth supporting."

After Darien fielded questions, Mrs. Evans introduced Safire, who opened her portfolio and summarized what the Law Offices of Benson and Hines planned to do for the Legal Assistance Program, selling the whole package along the way. Darien was seeing Safire in action in the professional arena for the first time. She was efficient but endearing, and she was very persuasive. He could see why Benson and Hines had sent her.

After that, Mrs. Evans introduced the potential backers by name and industry, and they each said a bit about what kind of corporate backing they did and why they were considering investing in the Heritage Center.

"I can't thank you enough for coming," Darien said.

Mrs. Evans went over a few pages in the proposal that Nova had helped to draft for the Heritage Center. "Now," she said, "I need to meet with the backers alone so we can create a response to the proposal. Don't go far, Mr. James and Ms. Lewis. We'll have our response ready within the hour."

Darien and Safire moved into the waiting area and dallied at the table set up with refreshments.

"What does she mean when she says that they'll create a response to the proposal?" Darien asked. "Does she mean that they're going to decide now who'll give what?"

"That's exactly it," Safire said. "These are the ones in charge, the ones who can make the decision."

"It might be good that I didn't know that going in," Darien said and then chuckled.

"Nervous, Mr. James?" She eyed him in a teasing manner.

"Well, there's a lot riding on this, like whether all those

kids have a safe place to go where they can learn something or get help. It's not about me. I'm incidental."

"You don't seem incidental."

Safire looked at Darien and gave him that seductive half smile. He couldn't tell whether she was making fun or not.

"Today you're standing in for the director of the Heritage Center," she said. "That's not incidental."

Safire had selected a pastry, and the sugar coating was all over her fingers, which she licked in the most alluring way. It reminded Darien of the sauce from the hot wings that she'd kissed and licked off his face in the sports bar, and the memory, paired with what she was doing now, made his body start to react. Was it him, or was everything about this woman erotic in some way?

They took seats in the waiting area, and Safire crossed one leg over the over, her long limbs showing in her short skirt.

Safire turned to him, genially placing her hand on his knee.

"So, Mr. James, are you still taking it slowly?"

"I guess I am," he said. "I've tried it the other way."

Her eyes flew open. "That says a lot about you. What about chicken and beef and lamb and pork? Have you gotten over your fear of meat yet? Or your fear of women?"

Safire's teasing tone made Darien look at her to gauge her intent. "I never said I was afraid of meat or women."

"Show me that you're not," she said, licking her fingers again.

Darien shook his head. "You don't slow down for a minute, do you? What makes you need to move so quickly? What makes you afraid of really having a man in your life, someone who knows you, someone who—"

Safire uncrossed her legs and recrossed them in a huff.

"I'm not scared, Mr. James. I just know what I want, and I'm not afraid to say it. You might be fearful of empowered women. I want someone who's not scared to go after what he wants and someone not spooked when I say what I want."

"You don't have to be wanton to have that, and you—"

"What if I like being wanton? Isn't it okay if I have desires and express them? If I were a man, you'd be giving me a high five, and we'd be bonding."

Darien couldn't help laughing at that, but he didn't agree.

"Not if you were a player. Not if you were seeking out one physical relationship after another."

Safire threw her arms up—literally. "Hold up. Hold up, Darien. Who on earth says that's what I do? That's not on any agenda of mine." She pointed her index finger up and followed her sentence with it. "So what makes that come into *your* mind? See, that's on you, sweetheart. You've tried it the other way, and maybe that's what you wanted."

"Oh, no—"

"I think so," she said and then laughed.

Without thinking about it, Darien cupped Safire's face in his palm, and she went silent.

"You don't have to put up a front with me, Safire. I've seen tears in your eyes. You're not all hot and heavy all the time."

With his palm under her chin, Safire stared into his eyes with her crescent-shaped pools. She was quiet for a long time, staring at him like that—frozen.

When he took his palm away, she leaned toward him.

"Come go out with me, Darien. Play with me. Let's see where it goes."

Her words were so quiet and her eyes so steadily trained on him that Darien almost thought he was hearing things. He paused a moment, his own breath caught in his chest. He righted himself and refocused. He was not hearing things. He'd never been asked out in such a sweetly alluring way.

"I have to work at the Heritage Center tonight," he said, unable to refuse the request but unable to honor it immediately. He was also troubled by Safire's phrasing. "And I don't know if I want to play—as you word it. I want something real. I—"

Just then, Mrs. Evans came out and beckoned them into the conference room. The group of backers had responded favorably to the proposal, and they had arrived at a collective response to the budget, covering all the basic programmatic needs. Mrs. Evans showed him a penciled breakdown and said she would fax the completed document over when it was all signed. This meant that the programs were secure.

It was more than Darien had dared to hope, and he was elated. He lingered to talk with some of the backers and thank them, and to let them know what else the Heritage Center was doing to raise the full amount needed for the larger operating budget—overhead, management and so on. Safire lingered to talk to them, as well. One by one, though, they began to leave after signing the completed forms.

Soon only one was left, a banker talking to Safire. Darien turned to their conversation only to find that it wasn't about the Heritage Center at all. The gentleman was asking Safire out. Darien looked at Safire, who was smiling her usual seductive, flirtatious smile with her butt propped up on the conference table much as she'd done with him when they'd met. She was slowly rocking her torso, and this only added to the seductiveness of her stance.

When she noticed him looking, she nodded and smiled his way and waited for his interruption before answering the invitation. Darien waved his goodbye, turned on his heel and headed to his car. Clearly, Safire was still playing the field, and when she had said *play,* that was what she had meant. Yes, this one was a seductress, but not only that. She was a player.

Darien got in his car and made it to the Heritage Center in time for his class, thinking all the while about Safire. She had seemed sincere, but she was just dating casually, if you would call it that. What bothered him was that he was actually miffed about it. He had no claim upon her. In fact, as they'd left it, he had turned down her invite to go out, by which she seemed to have meant *tonight*. Why should it rub him the wrong way if she took up another invitation from someone who was willing to play?

Darien pulled into the Heritage Center parking lot and got to his class, which comprised the little kids today—the ones who were between five and ten. He managed to focus on his class, but not without some distraction. Thankfully, they were molding shapes out of clay and didn't require a great deal of his concentration once they had selected their subjects for the project. The clay kept them in their seats and occupied, if not clean, and he had only to tour the room looking at projects and offering tips.

When the hour and a half was over and the children's projects were stored in the kiln to be fired, Darien greeted their parents. Mrs. Watson clacked in on her high heels wearing a short wraparound dress to pick up Jacob, an eight-year-old student. After she found out about his progress and collected her son, she clacked back out.

Her heels didn't make an impact the way Safire's heels did. They weren't seductive. They didn't show off long, shapely calves. They didn't announce her presence to the world. If anything, the sound struck him—at least today— as a nuisance. Nor was her short dress a distraction. Paired with her gaudy earrings and fake weave, it made her look more like a hoochie mama. Yet Darien knew that he was merely reacting to his departure from Safire and her willingness to entertain an invitation from another man.

Once his students left, Darien found the director of the Heritage Center, Mr. Abraham Johnson.

"Hey, Mr. Johnson."

"Abe."

"Yeah. That's what I meant."

Darien had been working at the Heritage Center since he started as a file clerk in high school, but the director was still Mr. Johnson to him, even now that he himself was an associate director.

"How'd it go today?" Mr. Johnson asked.

"Great," Darien said.

"I know."

"Did Mrs. Evans fax over the signed forms with the figures from the backers?"

"Yes, she did." Mr. Johnson stopped outside his office and raised his fists in victory. "We should celebrate."

"We should. Oh," Darien said. "I haven't talked to you since last week. You're a busy man."

"Not as busy as you, but then I'm not as young as you."

If Darien guessed correctly, Mr. Johnson was in his early sixties, but it didn't show much. Mr. Johnson just liked to have someone to whom to delegate the legwork.

Darien followed him into his office. "Did you get the letters of confirmation that I collected from Benson and Hines?"

"Yes, I got those, too. You've been productive."

"I already have clients signed up for the Legal Assistance Program for the next three weeks."

"What are their issues?"

"Some of everything you might imagine—condo conversions, divorces, child custody or child support, spousal battery, even one criminal charge."

Mr. Johnson turned to Darien and put a hand on his shoulder. "You know as much as I do now. When I'm ready to step down, my position will be yours."

"I don't know if—"

"It'll be a while, son. Just start thinking about it."

Darien nodded and left Mr. Johnson's office. Moving up at the Heritage Center wasn't what was occupying his mind. She was. Safire Lewis.

Darien had reading to do for his class on Wednesday, so he headed home. She was in the fast lane, and he'd gotten off that track—and for a reason. Besides, he couldn't satisfy anyone who needed to go out all the time. Nor could he be satisfied by anyone who still needed to play the field—or to act as if she was still playing it. Man, this one was someone to be wary of. He'd been burned by her type before. So why was he still thinking about her?

At home, even his reading was disrupted by the thought of Safire. He had started an erotic piece that he knew was inspired by her. It was still in the drawing stage, but it would be a wood sculpture. He put down his book for his class in Caribbean art and went over to his sketches. It was the sensual nature of the piece that let him know Safire had inspired it. And this irked him to no end. He wanted to put her from his mind. But here she was—his muse.

The piece had gotten inside his head, and he had to finish it. If he could finish it, if he could capture the spirit of her in a piece, he could release her from his mind. It was really because she had entered his art that she continued to occupy his thoughts. Or was it?

Chapter 3

Safire parked, grabbed her briefcase and started toward the Heritage Center. She was wearing a skirt suit, as usual, but this one was made of a shiny turquoise shantung blend. The jacket flared out at the waist and cuffs, and the mini-skirt flared at the hem. She had on her black pumps, and the heels tapped out her approach.

This afternoon she was representing Benson and Hines in the Legal Assistance Program. There were so many people seeking help that the firm decided to have her put in some time on the project doing preliminary interviews. This way, she could do a portion of the initial research and set up appointments for the clients with the right attorneys.

It had been two weeks since Safire had last seen Darien James, and she didn't know if she would run into him today. They were so different that she hadn't planned to pursue it any further. In fact, she hadn't known she would see him at the Nova Investment Firm meeting. He said he did a little administrative work at the Heritage Center, not that he stood in for the director at important fund-raising meetings. Well, plan or no plan, she might see him again today, perhaps if he was teaching an art class.

She didn't know how she'd feel if she did see him, but then, she didn't know how she'd feel if she didn't. She remembered the first day that she met him and the way he'd kissed her at her car. He was so firm, so gentle, so unlike everything she had known. And there was that moment at the investment firm when he'd cupped her chin and looked into her eyes. There was something about him in those moments, this tenderness. It just arrested her, froze her, threw her off-kilter. It didn't shut her down, but it immobilized her and halted her play. And it wasn't just because he was so sinfully good-looking.

Then again, Darien James was still a nondrinking, nonpartying, veggie-burger-eating stick-in-the-mud. Chocolate hottie though he may be, he was still too conservative for her. He wanted her to slow down rather than quench her needs, and she wasn't having it. Slow just wasn't her pace.

Safire opened the door to the main office at the Heritage Center only to find that there was no one at the receptionist's desk. Offices surrounded the reception area, but most of the doors were closed. She listened for a moment and heard no signs of movement, so she called out.

"Hello. Is anyone here?"

"Just a minute," a voice called back.

Then Darien's head popped out of a door. He had a phone to his ear and gestured for her to wait. Then he strode out from the office. He was wearing black jeans and a black T-shirt with a white shirt on top of it, and over that he wore a silver vest with words like *freedom* and *respect* embroidered in black thread. Around his neck he wore a leather rope with wooden beads that had a fist handing down at the center. Safire looked at him and couldn't help smiling. Now that he wasn't wearing a suit, he looked the part of an artist. His long braids were tied back at the nape of his neck, as usual, and his astute brown eyes stood out among his chiseled chocolate features, good enough to nibble on.

"Ms. Lewis," he said and held out his hand as he approached her.

"Mr. James," she returned. "Why so formal?"

"I didn't want to make any assumptions."

"Safire is just fine. I'm here to—"

"To do the interviews for the Legal Assistance Program. I know. I'll be serving as your staff liaison this afternoon, and you'll be using my office."

"Oh, I didn't know. Your office?"

"Come with me."

Safire had grown up in North Miami and had come to a few events at the Heritage Center, but she'd never been inside the administrative suite.

Darien led Safire to his office, which held a large wooden desk and two facing chairs with another chair in the corner. There were paintings of every kind all over the walls, some clearly by children. The shelves were lined with art books and sculptures made of wood and clay and ceramic. There was color in every conceivable corner. The file cabinets were covered with images—mostly watercolors—held on by magnets. Around the room were framed posters of events that had been held at the Heritage Center.

In addition to a computer and printer, the desk was strewn with papers, books and various art supplies.

"I just have to get a few things that I'll need out front, and I can make some room for you to work," Darien said, gathering things and clearing a space for her. "The first clients are in the small conference room across the reception area. I'll bring them in when you're ready, and I'll be at the reception desk to greet the next ones. We set appointments at the top of each hour, and you have four this afternoon." He nodded at her. "Just let me know when you're ready."

Darien took his things and went out to the reception area.

Safire pulled her portfolio and the needed paperwork out of her briefcase, including interview checklists, legal glossaries, a notepad and a pen. She spread out her things and made herself comfortable at the desk. Then she got up to find Darien.

"Is your receptionist off today?"

"We don't actually have a receptionist right now. We have a couple of student assistants, but they come in after school in time to service the after-school programs. We all do a bit of double duty around here. Are you ready?"

"Yes, I am."

Safire winked at Darien and headed back to his office. In a couple of moments, he brought in a family of three—two parents and their son. The son, who was fourteen, had been beaten up by a bully at school. The family was struggling and had no health insurance, and they wanted to sue for medical and dental fees resulting from the incident.

Anything involving children moved Safire's heart, filled her with conviction and focused her on the task at hand. This was the kind of case she wanted as her own, the kind of case she would study law for.

Having a little brother—one so much younger than she was—helped inspire that passion. She would have a fit if anyone was picking on little Philly. In reality, she had stepped out of the way to make sure that her older sister could look after her younger brother after their mother died. Angelina had to be free to concentrate on Philly. That was another reason she was on her own. She had to make sure that she was all right so that Angelina could go on making sure that Philly was all right. In fact, she had to be ready so that when Philly went off to college, she could pitch in when needed. So far, her plan was working, but it took grit and determination. And it took even more to have a life on top of that. It took being fierce. Now she wanted to go back to school. Hopefully, this plan would work, as well.

With only an hour, Safire had to make good time, so she let the young man describe the incident and then launched into questions. Near the end of the hour, she took their contact information and said that she would call them with an appointment for the proper attorney. She got up to shake the parents' hands and give the young man's shoulder a gentle squeeze.

"I'll be calling you tomorrow," she said and then smiled.

Darien came in to see if she was ready for the next client. She gestured toward the nearest chair and continued with her notes.

"I need to make some brief notes after each interview. It's standard practice. I'll only take five to ten minutes. That's why I ended a little early. Next time give me an hour and a half—at least—for each interview. In fact, it might work best if you call me with a general description of the issue when you're scheduling so I can estimate how much time I'll need."

Darien had taken the seat she'd pointed to. He propped one of his ankles on top of the other thigh and settled back. "We can do that."

Safire finished her notes and checked her watch. She had a few minutes to spare, and with Darien so nearby, she was itching to play for just a little bit. This wasn't like her. She liked to play, but not at work. Something about this man drew her to the chase. She tucked her notes into a folder, labeled it and stowed it in her briefcase. Then she got up and rounded the desk, settling back against it and crossing her legs in front of her.

"Are you ready for the next client?" Darien asked.

"Almost," Safire replied. "Tell me a little about them. Or do you know?"

"This one I do. Miss Levita Smalls has had her daughter in programs at the Heritage Center for about two years."

As Darien talked, Safire bent forward and touched the lettering on his vest, running her hand over his shoulder and down his chest as she read the words she was tracing with her fingers. He sat up in his chair but continued talking about Miss Smalls.

"She's been divorced for the last year and is struggling to keep afloat financially."

Safire bent farther forward, resting her hands on Darien's open thighs. With her so close, his voice quieted to a low bass.

"She works in housekeeping in a hotel in Coral Way."

Safire leaned in and kissed Darien softly on the cheek. Then she whispered in his ear, "What's her issue?"

Darien cleared his throat and turned to look at her. Safire leaned back up and folded her arms in front of her.

"She needs child support from her ex-husband."

"Bring her in."

Darien got up and went to the door. He looked back at her for a moment. His brow furrowed in consternation, and he shook his head. Then he disappeared.

Safire wasn't quite sure what had gotten into her. She never wasted time with anyone who wasn't entirely interested, and she was generally good about not mixing work with recreational pursuits, not while on the job. But here she was, tantalized by this man and wanting to tantalize him. Of course, he was sexy as hell. But there was more. There was a reservation about him and a sweetness. That was just as much a turn-on as his good looks and the way he could make her stop breathing by touching her face or kissing her. She wanted to take that self-righteous glint from his eyes and corrupt him. He kept her thinking about chocolate. *Oh la la.*

Darien came back with Miss Smalls, a petite woman in a blue floral dress. It was clearly her Sunday best, but it was fraying a bit at the seams, as was her handbag. Safire greeted her, showed her to a seat in front of the desk and settled in to do the interview.

"So, you're interested in suing your ex-husband for child support, Miss Smalls?"

"Yes, I am. He hasn't helped with Amelie since the divorce."

She needed to know about the divorce settlement and child custody ruling, about the ex's income and current family situation. She only had an hour, so she put aside other thoughts and focused.

When it was over, Darien came in and took a seat while she finished her notes.

"You know," he said, "you're really a nymph. But then, the way you dress kind of gives that away."

Safire snapped back, "First, thank you for the compliment. Nymphs were deities, as you know. And second, I am the girl next door, as long as you don't live next to a nunnery." She laughed and finished a sentence she'd been writing and then looked at him. "And you, you're the mild-mannered Clark Kent."

"Thank you."

"Oh—" she started on her notes again "—but what I want is a Superman."

"I think you're defining 'Superman' by the wrong paradigm."

"I beg to differ, not that you know what my paradigm is."

"I could describe it," Darien said, "but I think I need to let you write your notes. The next client is here."

Safire finished her notes and then looked up.

"Tell me about this one."

"This is Mrs. Martinez. I don't know a lot about her issues, only that there seems to have been some abuse in her marriage. I think she's moved out, but I'm not sure if they're divorced. I know that she's concerned for her children—there are two that I know of—and that she wants custody of them."

As always, when there were children involved, Safire refocused immediately. So far, all the cases at the Heritage Center had involved children, and it got Safire thinking about law school and specializing on cases with children. When she was finished, she would be great as a pro bono attorney for the Heritage Center. That or teaching children. She had to make up her mind, and she had to do it soon.

Safire looked up to find Darien staring at her.

"What are you thinking?" he asked.

Safire let out a breath. "I was thinking about how many of the cases here involve a threat to children. It's a shame. It's something I want to help fix."

"You are helping."

Safire didn't want to say more about her hopes for the future. "I know," she conceded. Then she looked at her watch. "Let's bring in Mrs. Martinez."

Safire did her interview, and then Darien joined her again as she wrote her notes. Because the interviews were so compacted, the hours were flying by for Safire.

"Are you getting anything done with all of these interruptions into your time?" she asked.

"A little. I don't work well with interruptions when I have real work to do. I can only multitask mindless work."

Safire looked up and smiled for a moment.

"You have a beautiful smile," Darien said, "and you smile often. I like that."

"Uh-oh. You're starting to sound enamored of a nymph. You better watch out or I might work my goddess powers on you." She chuckled.

"Speaking of you," he said, "how was your date with that banker you met at Nova?"

"I didn't have a date with him, but you sound a little jealous. That must mean you like me." She chuckled again.

Darien was quiet, and Safire finished the last sentence of her notes before glancing up. He was looking at her intently. Then he shifted and drew a folder from his lap.

"I've looked at the next set of interviews," he said, "and I've jotted down what I know about the cases. If you take a look when you're done, you can let me know how much time you'll need so we can reschedule."

They were looking at each other as he leaned forward, but when their hands met over the folder, they both looked down, suspended in the middle of a simple gesture.

Safire felt electricity in their touch. It moved from her hand to the pit of her stomach, and from there it crawled up her spine and wound down to the place where her body had started to throb. They both stood at the same time, facing each other across the desk. Safire looked back up at Darien, and what she saw in his eyes was desire.

It wasn't in Safire's character to back down from desire. It wasn't in her to let something go that she wanted without at least trying for it. She'd watched her sister become matronly under the pressure of being mother and father to their younger brother and a caretaker for their elderly great-aunt, who had recently passed away. Safire wasn't going to get old before her time. She'd learned to contend with the powers that be when they told her she couldn't—couldn't get along without a mother and father to help her make decisions, couldn't make it through college on her own, couldn't have a good life on only her income, couldn't do all that she wanted to do. That backbone she carried into all of her dealings. That pluck had become second nature.

Now she stood looking at the desire in Darien's eyes.

Safire spoke on impulse, "Come out with me tonight, Darien James."

Darien paused for a long moment. Then he sighed, and his brow wrinkled. "It doesn't seem to be in the stars for us, Safire Lewis, aka nymph."

"Why is that?"

"You mean in addition to how different we are? I have to work this evening. I'm teaching an art class in the after-school program after I bring in your last client, which I need to do now." He looked over his shoulder. "A student assistant will be out front when you're done. You can call me about rescheduling the next set of interviews." He turned toward the door and then turned back. "Take care, Safire."

Safire tipped her head and smiled.

In a moment, Darien was back with the last client and then took his leave. The man he brought owned a small business that was just beginning to break even. He was having trouble with a contractor hired to do some renovations for expansion. The job had been botched, but the contractor blamed the subcontractor and refused to fix it or pay for it to be fixed. Safire refocused and got through her interview. Then she packed up her things and waved to the student at the receptionist's desk as she headed out.

There was life in the halls now. People were on their way to various activities. Rooms were being used for tutoring, workshops, music lessons, art class.

Safire paused near a room where small children were engaged in what seemed to be an art class. She listened for Darien's voice, and when she heard it, she peeked inside. The scene was one of mild chaos. She saw empty chairs for bigger children at the back of the room. One was near her and partially obscured by the open door. She tiptoed inside and took a seat.

On observation, there was some order to the anarchy. Children with protective aprons tied about them and large goggles on had flat slabs of clay in front of them, which had been cut into four-inch tiles. Darien was instructing them on how to make decorations in the tile.

"They don't all have to be the same. If you want them to be similar, that's fine, but each will have some variation because these are handmade. Go to the front to look at the pictures if you still need more ideas."

He walked around giving the littler ones assistance and commenting on the pieces being made by the bigger children. Ages seemed to range from four or five to ten or twelve.

"Look at Kathy's. You can make holes in them if you'd like. That's fine. If you make a mistake, you can build the tile back up, but make sure not to leave seams. A bit of water helps. If you engrave the tile by drawing a design in it, use water to soften the edges of the engraving."

Darien was circling the room and was now in a position to see her. Safire wasn't sure what to do. She remained where she was, and he might have missed her except that while he was busy giving comments to one of the older boys, one of the younger girls came over to Safire. She might have been five, and she approached with a slab of clay plastered to her hand.

"Are you our teacher, too?" the little girl asked.

Her query drew Darien's attention, and he began watching them.

"No, little one, I'm visiting your class today."

"Look," the girl said, holding out her tile. "This one is a woman. I can't get it."

"That's very good," Safire said, "but if you draw in a dress here—" she used her finger to gently trace on the tile "—then it will look more like a woman, if that's what you like. It can be anything you want, and it doesn't have to look like what other people think a woman is."

The little girl ran back to her space at the table and used a blunt stick to etch in the line that Safire had traced. Then she ran back to Safire.

"Look, look! How's this? It's a woman now."

"That's very nice. Are you going to decorate the dress? You could draw little flowers or—"

"I'm going to use the thing to make dots," she said and took off again to her seat.

Darien kept circling the room and punctuating it with comments, but he nodded and smiled at Safire for a second, letting her know she had done okay. Safire was glad to have done a good job. She relaxed then and enjoyed the class until it was finished.

"Okay, all of your tiles should be nearly done. When you're finished, bring your cardboard with all the tiles and put them on the shelf to dry. I'll fire them in the kiln, and next class we paint them, so you'll be wearing aprons and goggles again." He laughed.

When class was over, parents or siblings came in to get the children, and they started filing out. Darien started on the cleanup and Safire got up to help.

"No way," he said. "Not in that outfit. You'll get this stuff all over you, unless you want me to wrap you in a plastic bag." He chuckled.

She settled back down and watched him.

"You handled Lucy well. You know, we always need help in our after-school programs. You have to get fingerprinted and all that, but it can be fun. You can assist a teacher with a class, or you can start your own in whatever specialty you have. And it doesn't have to center on little kids. We have programs for folks all the way up to adults."

"I'll have to consider the idea. It looks like fun."

Actually, Safire had already made up her mind. She wanted to know more about working with young people—teaching them. Her desire to work with children had her torn between law—with a focus on children—and teaching—with a focus on literature. She was already exploring law, but Darien's comment had just given her a way to explore teaching—working with young people directly. She was secretly thrilled by the possibility. But she didn't want it to be Darien's class, and she wasn't planning to launch a new class as a way of getting to him. She would call the director the next day and make arrangements on her own. Darien might not even have to know.

When he was finished, Darien turned to her. "Since

you stayed through my class, I'd like to invite you out for dinner."

"That sounds good, but let me call my girls. We had talked about a club tonight."

"While you do that, I'll go put things back in my office and collect what I need."

Safire made a quick call and was waiting for Darien when he returned.

Darien knew of an Italian place nearby where he could order vegetarian lasagna, so they went there for dinner. Safire had regular lasagna. She teased Darien with a forkful, and he teased her with a forkful of his.

"It's much sexier when you tease me," Darien said. "But no meat for me."

"Don't you miss it?"

"Sometimes. But I feel healthier this way. Only my mom can really tempt me on that front."

"Do you ever surrender to temptation?" Safire asked, turning her head and looking at him suggestively out of the corner of her eye.

"I'm not sure which question to answer—the one that you asked or the one that you implied."

They both laughed.

Over dinner they talked about his work at the Heritage Center and her work at Benson and Hines and where they overlapped. It went so well that they decided afterward to go to a place called Aunt Joe's, which had wine and coffee as well as foods and desserts. It had music videos playing on monitors and even dancing, though the floor was small.

Over his chai tea latte and her merlot, they split a piece of carrot cake.

"I guess this answers your question about me being a strict vegetarian."

"How so?"

"Latte and carrot cake—milk and eggs."

"You must have a sweet tooth," Safire speculated, thinking again of chocolate and how sweet this man would be on the palate.

"I do," Darien said. "But I don't do this often, and when I cook, I use substitutes."

"So you do give in to temptation sometimes." Safire winked at Darien and smiled, wondering if she could get her name added to the menu.

Suddenly, Safire asked Darien to dance. A slow song had come on, and she didn't want to miss a chance for a slow dance with this man.

There were few couples on the dance floor because it was so early, but Safire didn't mind. Darien, though, seemed a bit self-conscious, at least at first. Safire pressed her body against Darien's and felt herself begin to throb. She wrapped her arms around his neck, leaned her head on his shoulder and sighed. She closed her eyes against the multicolored strobe lights that circled the room and gave in to the sensation of being in Darien's arms. Although they were in public, it felt so erotic, so intimate, so safe.

The rugged smell of Darien's body filled her senses when she inhaled, and the taste of bittersweet chocolate rose to the tip of her tongue. The feel of his body was delicious. Their thighs brushed gently against each other's as they wavered to the slow, heavy beat and the guttural voice of a woman yearning for love. His hard chest pressed against her breasts, and his hands gripped her hip and back, drawing her into the curves of his form. It all sent a tingling through Safire that made her pulse rush. And she could tell from the bulge pressing against her hip that he was also getting a bit stimulated.

The slow song ended and a faster song came on. The two continued to sway slowly for a moment, long enough for Safire to know that he, too, hated to have the dance end.

Then they looked at each other and went back to their table, Darien's palm pressed to her back.

At their table, Safire placed her hand in Darien's. He accepted it and held it in a gentle fist.

She leaned toward him and motioned for him to come. He leaned his ear toward her, but that wasn't what she wanted. When she said nothing, he turned to look at her. That's when she caught his lips with hers. It was a chaste kiss, but they held it for a long moment before he leaned back, breaking the connection.

As she ran her fingers along his palm, he peered at her, but it was a gaze of inquiry.

"Why do you move so fast?" Darien asked.

"Well, I know what I want. What's wrong with that?"

"And what do you want, Safire?" He looked at her deeply.

She answered quietly, almost wistfully. "Come home with me, Darien." When he stalled, she looked him up and down and added, "I dare you."

Then she leaned back in her chair, crossed her legs and gave a devilish smile—waiting.

Chapter 4

Darien saw the challenge in Safire's eyes, her smile, her posture, her very being. And it was a challenge that he couldn't resist. It wasn't only that he was filled with desire for this woman. It was also that her defiance incited something in his masculine constitution. He had been triggered by his prey the way the canter of a deer sets a lion in motion. Desire and instinct were overruling reason and wisdom. He covered their tab, took Safire's hand and led them to her car.

"I'll follow you home."

Safire smiled like a kitty that had just found a stash of catnip. "Honk," she said, "if I get too far ahead of you."

"That won't happen," Darien said. "Just drive."

It wasn't until they were well on their way that Darien wondered what the hell he was doing and why on earth he was tossing his calculations out the window. His mantra had been that he would take things slowly until he found the right one—for sure. Now he was following a Cheshire cat to her lair. The thought made him laugh.

He parked beside her in the lot of a large apartment building off of Biscayne Boulevard in North Miami, and they went up to her apartment. She let them in and turned on a light and faced him, but he didn't take her into his arms. He took her elbow and started walking around her apartment, looking at where she lived.

"You live here alone?"

"Yes, I do."

"It's spacious."

It was all he would have expected for a chic, upcoming professional. There was a long, beige leather sectional in the living room with a matching love seat and armchair. These were accented by matching glass end tables and a glass coffee table. The books on the coffee table were eclectic—a pictorial history of Bob Marley, a photograph collection by James Van Der Zee, a visual encyclopedia of African-American history, a copy of Toni Morrison's latest novel, a few fashion magazines. There was a fully stocked entertainment center, and near it was a credenza with a bar on top. In the corner was a small bookshelf, but he couldn't read the titles from where he stood. The living room was sleek, smart and sparse. Everything was tasteful and elegant.

There wasn't much art. There was a charcoal drawing of a robust female nude and a watercolor of what looked like the harbor. There was a large, framed photograph of a Harlem scene from the 1920s, probably a Van Der Zee. That was it in the living room. To the left he could see the dining room, which had a fully set six-place table and matching chairs, but he couldn't see the walls without the light. Everything was clean and polished. It barely looked lived in.

"You like James Van Der Zee," Darien said, stepping around the couch to the path behind it, where the photograph hung on the wall.

"Among others," Safire answered, putting her purse on the credenza and coming to stand next to him. "I could afford them. They're just reprints."

"They're nice. I like his stuff, too."

Safire had been patient for a while. Now she put her

hands on Darien's chest and backed him against the wall. She pressed her body against his and put her lips against his throat.

Automatically, both of Darien's arms surrounded Safire's body, moving over the silky turquoise material that covered her back and flared at her hips. In her heels, she was just under his height, and he could feel the way her body stirred against him. When he dipped his head, he could smell the floral aroma rising from her earlobe. But what were they doing?

He lifted his head and cupped her hips, using them to move her back from his body. "You know, we don't have to move so quickly."

"What if this is what I want?" Safire asked.

"Is it?"

"Yes. What do *you* want?" Safire placed a hand on Darien's chest and moved it down his abdomen to the front of his jeans. "You seem to want me."

"I'm just saying—"

Safire took a step back. She put her hands on her hips and looked at him with one lifted eyebrow, as if waiting for him to show some moxie. Darien took a breath and shook his head. He was about to step around her when she pressed her body against his again and whispered into his ear, "I double dare."

Safire's soft voice in his ear and her soft body pressed against his lit Darien on fire as much as her demand. The deer was on the run again, and the lion in him was roaring.

Darien pulled Safire against him roughly, lacerating her body with his own. He dipped his head to her neck and sucked in the tender hollow, raising her against him until she was murmuring and rubbing herself along his body. The fire she had lit moved through both of them, and he was consumed by the flames.

"Is this that you want, Safire?"

"Yes, Darien, yes."

They moved toward her bedroom, tearing off each other's clothes as they gripped each other's bodies—her hands at his chest, his fingers on her breast, her mouth latching onto his throat, his palm cupping her rear.

By the time they reached the bed, they were down to their underwear, and Safire's tender flesh clung to Darien's hard body.

Darien stopped at the bed and broke from Safire. He needed to catch his breath and get his perspective back. Something about the fire in this woman was making him get ahead of himself, far ahead.

"Cold feet, *mon ami?*" Safire said.

"You know, we haven't even kissed properly yet," Darien said.

"Yes, you kissed me at my car the first day we met."

Yes, Darien thought. What had gotten into him then? Whatever it was was getting into him again. But tonight it was the dare in her eyes, the threat of fulfillment written in each of her movements.

"And our lips touched at the restaurant," she added.

"I don't know if I'd call that a kiss," he said.

Safire smiled and licked her lips. Darien could tell that she was about to show him what a real kiss was.

"Are you sure this is what you want, Safire?"

"It would be nice," she said, "if you're man enough to bring it."

Now the lion raged.

Darien lunged for Safire, pulling her bra down to expose her breasts to his lips as he moved his hand between her thighs. She touched him through his boxer briefs, feeling the length of him, the thickness. He moved his fingers into the thin, wet cloth between her legs and stoked the slick, swollen nub he found there. She moaned and gyrated against his hand while he felt himself leaping against her fingers.

When Safire stopped and pushed his hand away, Darien was startled.

She moved to his ear, licking the lobe before she whispered in it. "Don't tease me anymore," she said, and moved from his arms. Soon a dim light appeared from the other side of her bed. Safire opened a drawer and began rifling through it. She pulled out a condom and tossed it toward him. Darien stepped out of his underwear as he watched Safire slowly stripping off hers. Everything about this woman was erotic, and it seemed to him that sometimes, she wasn't even aware of what she was doing. The moment he rolled on the condom, his Cheshire cat pounced onto the bed and began stalking toward him.

Darien met her on the bed. He lowered her head to the pillow, spread her knees and placed himself between her thighs. With one hand under her shoulders, he used the other to grab hold of himself and run himself up and down between her dripping cavern.

"Don't tease you anymore?" he said, still teasing her.

Safire whimpered, and her hips oscillated. She grabbed her breasts and began to caress them, moving herself in time to his rhythmic stroking.

"No, Darien, please," she whined, and undulated. "Please, Darien, please."

Seeing her hands moving over her own breasts, paired with the feel of her hips, pushed Darien to the brink of control. It had been a while for him, but he knew something about pleasing a woman, and this one had told him to bring it. Bring it he would.

Darien moved slowly into Safire's body, feeling her tighten around him and hearing her suck in her breath and then murmur. She felt so tight, so wet, so sweet. He groaned and began thrusting gently inside her.

"Harder," she said once she had adjusted to his presence.

In response, his body began to gallop with hers. He brought one of his hands between them and added it to hers, moving it over her breasts. His Cheshire cat purred. Darien tilted his hips and circled them on the upstroke.

"Oh, yes," she said. "Right there."

"Here, baby?"

"Yes, please," she said, and then she cried out, continuing to move with him.

Darien moved this way until Safire took a breath and opened her eyes. It was then that he realized he'd been looking at her all along. They both paused, gazing into each other's eyes. Then, for the first time that night, Darien claimed Safire's lips. Her mouth opened beneath his. His tongue entered her mouth, and he felt her suck him inside. Their kiss started as a gentle pressure, but then, as Safire's lips opened for Darien, it became heavier, fuller, harder and more possessive. This kiss changed the tempo, the texture, of their union.

Something new was happening between them. Darien's body twitched, and he was propelled farther inside Safire's body. Her hips responded to the call, and they began moving together again. But with their lips locked together, the movement between them became richer, denser. Darien's advance was stronger, deeper. Safire's return was more eager, more forceful. They had become more inflamed but at the same time more tender. Their joined lips held them at the verge of passion, thickening their need but denying its resolution. Their wedded lips drew them to each other and tightened their embrace, connecting them to each other even as it drove their carnal urges.

Safire pushed Darien upward and moved her hand between them. Darien leaned up on his elbows and watched as she moved her hand over her sex and began kneading it. While she toyed with herself, she plunged in answer to his hips, sobbing out her rapture. Darien fought to retain his mastery but couldn't stop the groan that moved up from his belly and poured through his mouth. This woman was driving him to his limit.

Safire called his name and pulled him down against her again, and as he latched onto her lips once more, he felt her riding harder and faster, making him lope to her pace. Darien tilted his hips, and Safire moaned into his mouth. He felt her womanhood clamp around his engorged member and struggled to keep command.

Safire called his name against his lips, and her body began to jerk onto his. Darien could feel the waves of her pleasure moving along his manhood, pushing him over the precipice at which he had been standing for so long. He winced and called her name as the culmination of their union thundered through him.

Darien kissed Safire as their breathing slowed. He had raised himself onto his elbows so as not to put his weight on her. He rubbed their noses together, and she smiled, making him chuckle. He raised himself and lowered his body back down next to her, and she curled up against him.

He was surprised. What had he been expecting? That she would push him out of the bed the moment it was over?

Instead, she smiled at him—a sweet smile—and pulled on one of his braids. She traced her fingers over his chest and then tapped his breastbone to get his attention.

"Yes," he answered.

"That wasn't so terrible, was it?"

"No. It was wonderful."

"For me, too."

They were quiet for a little while as he stroked her back. He could look about her room now. In the dim light, he could see that it was more used than the front rooms. There were shoes piled outside the closet where she'd kicked them off, and clothes hanging on the closet door. There was another bookshelf across the room, and it was stacked with books and files of papers. There were knickknacks on her dresser, some art prints on the walls. They were on a large, floral comforter, and the matching pillows were on the chair next to a small desk, where her computer sat. This room was less posh and more girlie than the others, and it was lived in.

Safire rustled in his arms and then leaned up on her elbow, breaking the quiet mood that had come over them.

"Truth or dare?" she asked.

"I don't think I can handle another dare right away," Darien answered. They both chuckled. "So I'll say truth."

Safire leaned back down, resting on his arm. "So, who made you think that women are tramps?"

Darien wasn't ready for that question. It was a real question. It required a real answer.

"I don't think women are tramps, Safire. But I have been burned a couple of times, really burned. I used to play the field—in high school, in college. I was a lot like you seem now—living the life, partying, playing around. Then I went out with one girl for almost two years. When I was a senior in high school, I found out that she was seeing someone on the football team. No goodbye, no 'I'm not serious about you,' no nothing. She was just playing the field like I had been. So I went back to playing. Then, right after I graduated from college, I was actually engaged for a while. She traded me for a BBB—a bigger, better brother. She was just playing the field like I had been."

Safire caressed his arm. "I'm sure he wasn't better than you."

"No," Darien said. "He was an idiot. But that's what she thought. I just got burned and burned out. And I decided that I wanted to wait until I found someone real, someone I could love—no more playing around, no more playing the field, no more women who just wanted to have a good time."

"So you shut down completely—can't have a good time, can't be with someone and see where it goes, can't be your sexual self, can't—"

"I didn't say that. I just decided to take things slower and not just play anymore."

They had talked more, or rather, Safire had gotten him to talk. Darien thought about that conversation now, while he was chiseling a piece of wood in the early afternoon. He hadn't spoken to Safire in four days, but that night, she got him to open up about things he didn't want to remember and thought he had forgotten.

He hadn't known it was so obvious that he'd been burned before. Maybe she just assumed he'd been burned because he wanted to get to know someone before heading to bed with them—at least now he did. He'd tried it the other way. It hadn't worked. If that was conservative, so be it. In fact, he hadn't planned to get intimate until he was reasonably sure that he'd found the right one. So what had he done with Safire?

Darien got a piece of sandpaper and started sanding the curve he'd just created in the walnut he was working with. He thought back to when he'd played the field in his younger days—meeting women, having casual encounters, letting things go wherever they went. That's not what it felt like with Safire—not at all. Their passion had been amazing, but he felt a connection there, too. He felt it while they were making love and when they were caressing each other afterward and when they were talking. But still, he was abandoning his own rules with her, and he didn't rightly know why.

Or rather, he didn't know fully why. She was beautiful, but that wasn't it; that wasn't what drew him to her and kept her on his mind. It was something else. It was the flashes of tenderness that swept over her—like those tears on the first night, or the stillness that came into her body when he cupped her chin, or the passion in her voice when she talked about how many of the cases at the Heritage Center involved children. He sensed something inside her that felt…like a hunch—sweetness lurking just under the covers, under the brashness and forwardness of her, even inside her Cheshire cat smile. He wanted to know that woman.

Instead, she had gotten him to talk about himself, and she had told him very little about her life. And now it had been four days.

Darien turned the wood he was working on and picked up one of his carving chisels and one of his mallets to start on another plane. They had slept in each other's arms and had gotten up Saturday morning late. He had to get to his Saturday-afternoon art classes for adults at the Heritage Center as well as his own artwork and then a paper for school. She had plans as well, but she didn't say what. They had a quick breakfast at a café near her place and parted with a gentle, telling kiss. She had given him that Safire smile—the sweet one—and told him she would be in touch. Darien didn't have her home number. He hadn't gotten hers when he entered his into her cell phone over breakfast. They'd been interrupted by the waitress. If it wasn't play for her, why the wait? Why hadn't she called?

Darien put down his tools and stepped back from the piece he was working on. He was in the second bedroom of his apartment, his workroom for his wood. It was filled with supplies, projects in process, finished pieces, tools, dust, wood chips, shavings—general bedlam. It took a little lawlessness to create art, any art.

Behind him was the piece he'd started after meeting Safire, and he turned to it. The sculpture was large to begin with, but it kept growing. He had started with large slabs of claro walnut. Now he was gluing Indian rosewood together for a base that was as wide as the claro walnut was tall. The central figure was now Safire, but being able to capture something of Safire's image wasn't curing him of the inclination to think about her. He'd thought about her all the more since their night together, and he had a yearning that wasn't just for her body.

Darien walked around the piece, testing the clamps and visualizing the figure that he would pull from the erratic form. He wanted to slow things down with Safire, get to know her, follow the path created by what he had already started to feel for her. But with each passing day, he was less and less sure that it was anything more than a one-night fling to her. What did she want? Or had he already seen the only thing she wanted? He had started wanting more, but maybe he was the only one. Maybe he should have stuck with his plan and not gotten physically involved until he knew he'd found the right one.

He turned from the piece. He couldn't work on it now. He had to change and run some errands before coming home to finish his work for classes the next day.

Amid his tasks, Darien stopped at two of the places that sold his work. One was an art dealership, and they had sold one of his pieces. This was good news; he was getting his name out there. The other was actually a lighting store. He made lamps from wooden carvings of African family trees—the ones with the elongated bodies of people connected one to the other that were made in Kenya and other countries. These were of the same flavor but with a flair all his own, usually in ebony or African blackwood or mahogany.

The lighting store carried samples of his lamps and took orders for him. When he stopped in, he found that they had just taken an order of six for him—six of the tall floor lamps with moderate detail. This changed how he could commit his time. He needed the exposure, so he would have to go into overdrive. He would have to budget his work on the Safire piece and ration the time he let himself ponder over her.

Chapter 5

Safire finished double-checking the bathroom cabinets and the closet and then sat on her couch to wait for her family to arrive to help her with the last leg of her move. She'd been moving the remaining small things. Everything was gone except the heavy stuff—the furniture. She had dollies all ready and just needed the extra hands.

Safire looked around her apartment. She would miss it. She was giving up living alone so that she could go back to school. With her sister getting married and becoming more financially stable, it seemed like a good time. No one knew as yet because she still had a lot to figure out, but this was part of the plan. She'd saved up money from working for a couple of years and could use student loans for the rest if she couldn't find scholarship money. But to tighten her budget, she had to give up her space. It was a smaller space or a roommate, and she'd decided on the roommate.

She was able to take advantage of an opening in her apartment building for a two-bedroom apartment. She had planned to find a woman with a similar sensibility to her own, hopefully a student at Florida International University, where she planned to go to school. But her super knew of someone he could vouch for. Her name was Janelle Hawkins, and she was also from North Miami. She was a little conservative, but they'd had a long talk and thought they could work things out.

She'd already checked, and when she was ready, she would be able to continue working part-time and during summers for the Law Offices of Benson and Hines. This would give her rent and living expenses. It should be okay. Now she only had to decide what she wanted to go to school for.

The original plan was law school with a focus on children's issues. As an undergraduate, she'd taken an English major and an Administration of Justice minor and had done her associates degree to be a paralegal on the side. She loved being a paralegal. Only now she wasn't sure that she wanted to study law. She had to decide about her true calling, which might be teaching. That was why she was starting to volunteer at the Heritage Center. She'd arranged it through the director, Mr. Johnson, and she'd even gotten the days when Darien was off, so he didn't even have to know about it.

Safire couldn't think of the Heritage Center without thinking of Darien and the night they'd spent together. She wished he would be coming today because she hadn't seen him in almost two weeks. But she needed a larger group and hadn't even had the time to call him with an invitation. She'd been busy packing and moving and doing lesson plans, and work was busy, too. That, however, wasn't the only reason she hadn't picked up the phone.

Being with Darien that night had been incredible, and being with him in general had been unlike anything she was used to. She had wanted him, but getting him was more than she had bargained for. He had rocked her world, and then he had rocked her in his arms. They'd spoken into the wee hours of the night, falling asleep in each other's arms.

Safire could imagine herself becoming attached in a way that wasn't her regular style, and if what he said was true, he might feel the same way. And as different as they were, that might not be a good thing. She wanted the new man in her life, but she had needed to slow things down—not physically but in every other way. Ironically, Darien had been right, not about waiting for sex but about not letting things get out of hand too quickly. She hadn't thought about it until now, but this was why she had delayed calling him—to cool things down.

When Safire heard the buzzer sound, she was lost in thought. She pulled herself out of it and let in her big sister, Angelina, who was a history teacher at FIU and who was followed by their baby brother, Philly, who had just turned seven. Straggling behind these two came their twenty-year-old cousin, Alex, and Angelina's fiancé, Jeremy, a radiologist she met on a cruise at the beginning of the year—the cruise that Safire was supposed to have taken but couldn't.

Safire hugged her big sister and patted her little brother's head.

"I didn't know you could walk without heels," Jeremy said as he hugged her.

Safire looked down at the sneakers she had on and pursed her lips. "Very funny. I only use these to exercise—when I do that. Don't mess with a black woman and her shoes now."

"Okay, Mrs. Imelda Marcos," Jeremy said.

"Hush now," Safire said. "Sistergirl had almost three thousand pairs of shoes. She must have needed a house for her shoes."

Safire, Jeremy and Angelina laughed.

"Thank you for the help, you guys," Safire said. "I couldn't get these by myself. The rest is done."

"I see," Jeremy said, "that being hardheaded and having to do everything on your own runs in the Lewis family."

Safire and Angelina glared at Jeremy while Alex silently smirked.

"But I'm not doing it on my own, am I?" Safire said. "It's just downstairs. And trust me. I'll call in for favors. Don't forget you owe me one already."

"I'm sure you will," Jeremy replied. "And this doesn't count. You'll be doing the same soon."

After their honeymoon, Jeremy and Angelina would be moving together to a new house midway between their jobs; of course, they would be bringing Philly and Alex with them. They were outfitting it now and would renovate the old house—the house Safire and Angelina grew up in—to sublet later on.

Jeremy and Alex each took an end of the sofa and headed out into the hall.

"Phillip," Jeremy called, "you can come with us."

With the boys gone, Safire's sister turned to her. "Safire, are you sure you want a roommate?"

Angelina knew her well, and Safire caught her meaning. Safire didn't want to tell Angelina about her plans for school until they were all settled—financially and otherwise—so she made it seem like a space issue. "Oh, I can still do what I want. It's perfect. Less rent, more space."

"How can you do what you want with a roommate?" Angelina asked.

Safire and Angelina each grabbed an end of the armchair, lifted it and headed into the hall.

"I can be discreet," Safire said, and she couldn't resist telling her sister more. "In fact, I think that there's a new man in my life. Maybe you'll meet him soon."

Bringing home her latest beau wasn't new for Safire. This time, though, she really wanted her family to meet Darien, not incidentally but because he mattered. Feeling this way confirmed for Safire that Darien seemed to be getting to her in a way that her other boyfriends hadn't, and that worried her a little. Once again, she considered that she might want to slow things down a bit—not physically—that wasn't her style—but in other ways.

"Anyone special?"

Yes, Angelina knew her sister.

Safire smiled to herself before she answered. "We'll see."

The next couple of hours were spent moving the furniture. Then Safire took everyone out for pizza. That night, she was staying with Philly and Alex so that Angelina could have some time alone with Jeremy at his place. She had been doing more of that recently—since their great-aunt had died and since Jeremy had come into their lives. It felt good to do her part to help take care of her little brother. Angelina was raising him because Angelina was older, but Safire could play a role, too.

After dinner, the group split up, and Safire took the boys to a movie before taking them home to the old house where she grew up. It was getting dark when they got in, so she got Philly set for bed, read to him a bit and then tucked him in.

She was spending the night in her sister's room and left Alex downstairs watching television so that she could get some work done. It made her imagine what her sister's life had been like all along—work, taking care of Philly, taking care of Aunt Rose before she died. Safire couldn't live that way, but then she didn't have to. Safire sighed, glad that she was doing more now to help out and glad that Jeremy was doing more to get his sister out of the house.

Safire hunkered down at Angelina's table with her knapsack to look over selections for her reading groups at the Heritage Center. Last week, she had done two sessions with the instructor who used to lead the reading groups. This week was her first time presenting book selections on her own. Her Tuesday-evening group was the older group, thirteen to sixteen, and they were reading the first installment of a novella about racial prejudice. Her Thursday-evening group was composed of the younger children, eight to twelve, and they were reading a short story about cultural differences.

Safire took a breath, wondering why she was so nervous about this. Why were groups of kids harder to anticipate than a group of hardened lawyers?

"I was an English major," she said out loud. "I can do this."

After she adjusted, if she wanted, she could even stay after and tutor in the Academic Enrichment Program. For now, leading two reading groups was enough. It cut into her work at Benson and Hines, which they didn't mind since her time was going to a worthy cause. But it also cut into her time with her girls and going out. She had thrown out her daily planner; she hated keeping schedules and being on timetables. Late nights at the law firm were more than enough. Now she might have to give in and get one so that she could keep up with her reading groups. And she would definitely need one when she started school again. Ugh.

Safire reviewed the texts she would be using with the kids, going over the parts she planned to have them read out loud in class and rehearsing her discussion questions.

She paused and was about to go check on Philly. He'd started having seizures earlier that year, and though his condition seemed under control, they needed to keep a close eye on him. As she got up, there a came a knock at the door. It was Alex.

"Come in."

Alex opened the door but hung back near the doorway.

"Is everything all right?" Safire asked.

"Yeah. Philly got up and wants to stay with me tonight. He says the movie scared him."

Safire smiled. They had seen an animated science fiction movie, but it did have scary alien creatures in it—scary for a seven-year-old child.

"That's fine. I was just going to check on him, but if you're going to bed, just keep an eye out."

"Yeah. You want his room tonight?"

"No, I need Angelina's table tonight. I brought a bit of work home with me. Hey, what about your online class in… animation graphics?"

"It's basic game graphics. It's going okay so far."

He didn't say more, as usual, so she left it alone, and they said good-night. Now she saw what Angelina had been up against all that time with their quiet cousin. She might not be much help on that front, but she could be of more assistance with her younger brother, and she was helping to plan her sister's wedding. She'd brought sample invitations to leave for Angelina, which she pulled out and deposited on the desk before she forgot.

Safire had also brought her application packets—one for law school and one for graduate school—and she started reviewing her personal statements. She wasn't long into it when she decided to stop and make the call she'd been wanting to make but putting off for almost two weeks. She took out her cell phone and called Darien.

"Hello," he answered, and the sound of his deep voice crept down Safire's spine.

"Hi, beautiful," Safire said, smiling and excited to talk to him. "I hope it isn't too late to call, but you said you were a night owl, so I decided to take a chance."

There was a long pause on the other line.

"Hello?" she called.

"I'm here," Darien said. "I'm just wondering why you're calling me after two weeks—almost two weeks. Why are you calling, Safire? Why has it taken two weeks?"

Darien's voice was sober, stern, uninviting. He was angry. And his anger doused Safire's excitement like a deluge. Still, he had something of a point; she would feel similarly if she'd been waiting for him to call. That meant he must have missed her, too.

"You didn't give me your numbers. Remember? So what is this?"

"I've been moving. I just finished today."

"You didn't seem to be packing when I was there."

"Exactly," Safire said. "I had everything to do."

"That doesn't explain why you couldn't find ten minutes in the past two weeks. You could have even called me to help you."

"I had it covered. It just took time. But I've wanted to see you again."

"Apparently not enough."

"Maybe too much," Safire admitted, not sure how to explain her delay.

"Haven't gotten enough of what you want?" Darien asked.

Now he was going a bit too far. "What do you mean by that?"

"I mean, is this something to you, or is this a booty call?"

Now he had gone way too far. Safire got to her feet. "You don't know me enough to imply what you're implying. *Don't* mix me up with your past fly-by-night flames." Her finger made an arc through the air, and her fist came to rest on her hip.

"Okay. Maybe I'm off base," Darien admitted. "But the point is that I don't know you well enough. I need to know you better."

Safire sat back down and leafed through one of her applications while coming out of her huff.

"Look," Darien said, "I didn't know what to think when I didn't hear from you all that time. It started to seem like it was just a casual thing to you. I used to play the field. Remember? And that's how I got burned."

"You told me about them."

"My point is that I see you doing what I used to do. I don't want you to get burned or burned out."

"I take care of myself pretty well."

"Maybe," he said quietly, "you should let someone else take care of you a little bit, too."

Darien's soft, deep voice sent a shiver through Safire. She purred and said, "I like how that sounds." Then she chuckled.

"I didn't mean it *that* way."

"Of course, Mr. Saint couldn't possibly have meant it *that* way. But I liked it *that* way."

"But that's not all there is, Safire."

"I never said it was."

"So let me know you better," Darien said.

The sincerity in his voice quieted Safire. "Okay, Darien. What next?"

After a long pause, he said, "Come with me somewhere. What are you doing now?"

Safire looked around her sister's room and toyed with the idea, but she couldn't run off when she was supposed to be watching Philly. "Uh, I'm previously engaged."

"What does that mean?" Darien asked.

"It means I'm out already," Safire said, hoping he wouldn't pursue the topic. She wasn't ready to tell him about her family. "How about tomorrow? I get out a bit late, but I can be ready by eight."

"You date a lot, don't you?"

"I like to get out, even if it's with my girls. But I guess I date a fair amount."

"Anyone serious?"

"Not really. I guess I never found the right one."

"Could it be me?" Darien asked.

"That's what we want to find out," Safire replied.

"Then tomorrow at eight."

They made plans for the next night; he would make

them dinner at his place, and he had just gotten a movie they could watch if it wasn't too late. She gave him her cell phone number, and he gave her his address. She would be meeting him at his place.

Safire clicked the phone closed, excited that she would be seeing Darien again.

Chapter 6

Darien put down his chisel, loosened the clamp holding the statue to the table, turned it over and clamped it down again. This piece was one of his family trees—the base for one of his lamps. On the other end of the table he had one of his pieces for school. It dominated the table. The broad strokes were finished. Now he had to do the detail work and relief.

In the corner under a canvas was the Safire piece. He had gotten to a stage where he didn't know how to go on. He had captured the erotic quality of Safire's character, but there was more there. There was also a sweetness that he had just begun to factor in. In fact, she was full of contradictions: tough but tender, independent but youthful, saucy but sweet. There was more to her in general, and Darien needed to know more so that he could figure out how to proceed with the piece. For now, he'd moved it to where she wouldn't see it; it wasn't ready to be seen.

He wouldn't be able to work on it tonight because it was seven, and she was coming at eight. He patted his clothes to get off some of the wood chips and sawdust, and then he went into the kitchen to pull out all the things he would need to make eggplant Parmesan—for himself—and chicken Parmesan—for her. When everything in the kitchen was ready, he went into his room, gathered his underclothes and hit the shower.

Darien wasn't sure what to wear for a date with Safire if they were staying in. His usual jeans and T-shirt didn't stand up well against the little skirt suits she wore all the time. He wanted to make an impression, so he opted for a pair of pleated navy slacks and a bright blue sateen dress shirt. He wanted a little something of himself, so over that he put on a multicolored vest, and he finished it off with his bronze-and-black sneakers.

When his buzzer rang, Darien let Safire into his apartment building and waited for her at the door. What he saw coming down the hall was not the Safire he was used to. Instead of her usual skirt suit, she had on a short cocktail dress. It was azure blue and hugged her curves up to her breasts, where it stopped, with one thin strap at each shoulder. Over the top was a small, sheer bolero top with rhinestones down the front, around the neck and at the cuffs. It stopped just below her breasts and was so translucent that it actually worked to show off what was beneath rather than conceal it.

She had on strappy silver sandals that were at least two-and-a-half inches high. Her toes were painted the same red as her fingernails, and her face was made up to the nines. The front part of her hair was pulled back into a barrette, but the back fell in curls down her back. She had a little silver purse in her hand and a wide smile on her face that was at once innocent and tempting. She was gorgeous.

While he gaped at her, Safire leaned up on her toes and gently kissed his lips. Like her smile, the kiss was both chaste and erotic. She hadn't even gotten in the door yet, and Darien was already starting to get inflamed.

"Hi," she said.

"You look beautiful," Darien said, drawing her into his

apartment. "You look like you're going out on the town. Maybe we should."

"No, we don't have to go out. I just like to dress for my dates."

"You look...stunning."

Safire smiled, twirled around and gave Darien a model-type pose. Then she laughed. "Thank you. You look nice yourself." Safire looked at him. "Are you still mad at me?" she asked and then made a little pout.

Darien had to be honest. "Well, I haven't forgotten that it took you almost two weeks to call me after I spent the night at your house."

"I know. I'm sorry. I had to move and... I won't let that happen again."

With some of the unspoken out in the open, Darien took a deep breath, smiled tentatively and gave Safire a brief hug. He still hadn't heard the real reason why it had taken so long. He still didn't know. He released her into his apartment, thinking once again that she looked as if she was going out.

"Are you sure you don't want to go out?" he asked.

"Yes, I'm sure," she said.

She was already wandering into the living room and taking in his apartment, which was generally the opposite of her own. Safire's space was streamlined and modern. Darien's was anything but that. He had art everywhere—on the walls, on his shelves and tables. It filled every conceivable space. Most of it was his own, but some of it was his students' work, and some of it he had just collected. There was also color and texture everywhere. His sofa and chairs had been reupholstered in African cloth, and he'd tiled over his wooden coffee table. He went for unique rather than posh, multicultural rather than modern.

His bookshelf was stacked with art books and school-books, and workstations were set up all over his apartment. The second bedroom was used for woodwork, but the breakfast nook was set up for clay, and half the dining room was set up for drawing and painting. Instead of a china cabinet, he had a shelf full of paints. Art supplies were everywhere except in his bedroom, which was the only rather normal room in the apartment. But even there, his bedspread and curtains were made of Ashanti kente cloth, and it was also rather covered in art. It wasn't that tidy, but then he didn't expect them to go into that room tonight.

"Your place is amazing," Safire said, still looking around. "I love all the art. Did you make all of these?"

"Some of them. I'll show you a few of my pieces after dinner. That's why I wanted you to come over—so I could show you my stuff."

"What I see is incredible."

Safire was looking at the African masks that Darien had around his entertainment center.

"Those aren't mine."

"I know. You have a lot of African art, don't you?"

"It inspires me."

"And lots of imagery of women."

"I guess that inspires me, too."

"You have lots of stuff," Safire said, coming to him. "You must have been living here awhile."

"Ever since college." With Safire standing right in front of him, Darien became a little self-conscious. "Do you want to wait here or to come into the kitchen while I cook us dinner?"

"I'll come. I can help." Safire saw the chicken laid out on the counter and gave Darien a brief kiss on the cheek. "Aw, you got chicken for me."

"Yes, I didn't know if you'd like eggplant by itself. I also got you wine—one red and one white."

For that he earned another kiss.

Darien was glad that his small considerations hadn't

gone unnoticed. But the fact that Safire had noticed and even that she'd thanked him pointed out the huge differences that still stood between them. And as she watched him pour olive oil into the frying pan, he was sure that they stood out in her mind, as well. But there they were, and she seemed happy to see him, as happy as he was to see her.

While Darien sautéed the eggplant and the chicken, Safire made their salad. When the sauces were bubbling, he put the pasta on. By the time he had set the dining table, everything was ready. He added Parmesan to Safire's chicken and served up their plates. Safire was looking at the art on the walls in the dining room and the painting station that took up the other half of the room as they started to eat.

"This is wonderful," she said.

"I'm glad you like it. I think that's actually a piece of the eggplant that I gave you," Darien said and then laughed.

Safire swatted his arm across the small table and chuckled. "Don't try to turn me vegetarian. I love meat—beef and pork and—"

Darien laughed. "Your eyes were glazing over."

"See what I mean?"

"Don't worry. It's not catching."

There they were again—their differences. Yet Darien could barely take his eyes off her, and there was so much that he wanted to know. Unfortunately, Safire was the one who made the first inquiry.

"Tell me about your family," she said.

"We're from here. I have one younger half brother. He's gay. He's a sweetie. My father died when I was little, and my mother remarried, so I have a little half brother. They were divorced when he was three, and we were raised by my mother here in Miami. She's a nurse."

"Was it hard on you financially? Is that why you're so keen on the work the Heritage Center does for those in need?"

Darien hesitated. He didn't like to flaunt what he had, but he wanted to be honest with Safire. "When my father died, he left me the value of his business. He owned a lumber-supply company. I'm pretty well situated, enough that I can help out the Heritage Center when I need to. Enough that I know I'll always be okay. I want to make it as an artist, but I'll never have to starve."

"So your father worked in wood, as well. That's nice. What about your brother?"

"My brother is in his fourth year as a psychology major at FIU. He'll be finished next May. We're all pretty close. My brother lives on campus, but we see my mom every other weekend or so." Darien stopped. He didn't want this to be like the other night, when he did all of the talking. "What about you? I know your parents are gone but that you have siblings."

"I have an older sister and a younger brother, and our cousin lives with them. We're from North Miami—born and raised."

"Are you close?"

"Kind of. I see them about once a week these days."

Darien felt Safire's toe moving up his leg. And there they were again—their differences. Fast versus slow.

"Are you playing footsies with me?" he asked and then laughed.

"Maybe. Do you like it?"

"You're incorrigible. And you're just trying to get out of having to talk about yourself. Why?"

Safire smiled, caught. Darien was starting to know her smiles, and he loved that and loved them. No differences between them could stop that.

"I don't know," she said. "I guess I tend to be a bit private."

"Tell me something private," Darien said, wanting so much to get inside this woman's mind.

"There isn't much."

"What? Tell me."

"I want to go back to school. I started out wanting to focus on children and the law, and now I'm not sure."

This wasn't terribly personal, but Darien could tell that it was personal to Safire. It was important to her and real for her.

"Tell me more," he said.

Safire shrugged. "That's all I know right now. I still want to work with children, but I'm not sure if it'll be through law or teaching or something else."

They had finished eating, and Darien reached across the table and took Safire's hand. "You'll figure it out. You'll find your way."

"I know," she said.

"Can you afford it on your own?"

Safire let out a breath, as if the tension had been broken. "That's another question. I've been saving for the last couple of years—well, except for clothes and shoes and going out."

They both chuckled.

"Other than that, I've saved a bit. I'm going to look for scholarships when I figure out what I want to do. And if that doesn't work, there are student loans. That's also why I moved."

"Why?"

"To save money. I have a roommate now, so we're splitting the rent."

"You couldn't move in with one of your siblings?"

"They live together. And no, I didn't want to do that. I've been on my own for too long. And they have issues of their own to deal with—financial and otherwise. They don't even know I'm going back to school yet."

Darien moved Safire's hand to his lips. "Thank you for telling me. I hope you tell me more about you. Will you?"

Safire nodded and smiled.

"I should have brought dessert," Safire said.

"I have dessert for us. The James household is never without dessert. It's my mom's apple cobbler."

"Now *your* eyes are glazing over," Safire teased.

They both chuckled.

Darien got their dessert à la mode.

"I just got a copy of Tyler Perry's *For Colored Girls,*" Darien said. "Did you see it?"

"Actually, no. But I read Ntozake Shange's original. I'm up for seeing it."

"Before that, I want to show you some of my art, if you'd like."

"Yes, I would."

Darien took a breath. He was always a little nervous showing his work, but this was special. This was Safire. He took her hand and led her to the bedroom that he used for his woodwork. Along the back wall, he had reinforced wooden shelves where he stored some of his pieces. He drew off the covers that he used to protect them, and Safire stepped forward.

"Oh, my God. These are amazing."

Safire walked along the shelving, touching the pieces and stopping to look at some of the more intricate ones. "These are so beautiful. The faces on the human figures are so real, and the detail is phenomenal. And some of these are huge. You work with everything, don't you?"

"Yeah, I add a little of everything to wood. Inlay, ceramic, paint, metal, glass, mosaic, stain, burning—anything I can do that seems to fit."

Safire was looking at his artwork but Darien was looking at her—the way she touched the pieces and when she stooped down to see the ones below, the way she tipped her head to read the name tags and when she turned a piece to see it more fully. He loved the way she peered into his inside life, and he loved the way she looked. Her azure-covered curves topped anything that he had done. All differences aside, he was drawn to this woman—body and mind.

"I'm putting together an exhibit, so I've been working on pieces. The family trees are going to be lamps. I sell these, but some of these kinds of pieces will go in the exhibit, as well. African art is functional. I want to include that tradition. The larger pieces are in the middle of the room. They won't fit on the shelves."

Darien uncovered some of the pieces that were on the floor, life-size pieces or larger, leaving the Safire piece covered in the corner. Then he leaned back against the wall and just observed her taking in his art.

After about fifteen minutes of just watching her, Darien took Safire's hand and led her to the bathroom—now a storage room. He flipped on the light, showing Safire his drawings, sketches and paintings.

"Wow. You're good."

"This isn't my main thing, but the better I get at this, the better my woodwork is."

"I see the African influence."

"And Caribbean and African-American and Italian and…more."

Safire flipped through some of the canvasses lining the walls and filling the bathtub. After a few minutes, Darien tapped her shoulder.

"There's one more stash."

Darien took Safire's hand and led her to the huge, walk-in closet that made him pick this room for his art. Inside he had more woodwork, but he also had his ceramic work and clay pieces—tiles, mosaics, freestanding sculpture.

When Safire was finished there, she reclaimed Darien's hand and went back to the woodwork in the bedroom.

"I can't get over how beautiful these are."

"We'll see how my exhibit does," Darien said. Still, he couldn't help smiling.

Safire came to him and put her arms around his neck. She pressed her body to his and kissed him. Darien had been wanting to feel those soft curves all night, and despite wanting to take it slowly, he couldn't help wrapping Safire in his arms and taking control of their kiss, moving his tongue into her warm mouth and pulling her more firmly against his chest. After some time, they broke the kiss.

"Show me your bedroom, Darien."

"Uh, I hadn't planned to go there tonight."

"Please," she whispered in his ear.

Darien's manhood leaped, and he pressed Safire against him. She reached down between them and began to massage the taut mound at his center. Darien couldn't help the way his body jerked under Safire's touch. What was it about this woman that made him abandon all his rules?

Safire took his hand, led them to the living room, where she collected her purse, and then drew him to the only room in the apartment that she hadn't been inside yet.

Darien stood watching Safire undress, wondering what about this woman moved him so much and why, given all that, he couldn't slow down with her. When she got down to a black strapless bra, black lace panties and silver sandals, Safire pulled a condom out of her purse and looked at him where he stood, fully clothed.

"Dare," she said. "No, double dare."

They smiled as he stepped across the room, lifted her onto his bed and climbed in after her, positioning his body over hers. She moaned as he rubbed himself along her body. Then she started pulling at his clothes.

They made love into the night, and then Safire curled toward his body, settling in his arms.

"I'm sorry, Safire," Darien said, thinking about what he had planned for that night.

"Sorry? That was wonderful."

"I'm sorry for letting it turn sexual when we were supposed to be spending time getting to know each other."

"Darien, it doesn't have to be one or the other."

"In principle, I agree. But in practice..." He didn't know how to say that with them, given the way she lit up his body, given the way he was drawn to her, given the way their chemistry seemed to obliterate other forms of interaction, it might just be one or the other.

"How about this?" he said. "What if we cool it down a bit and get to know each other more outside the sheets, vertically, that is?"

"Hmm," she murmured. She pressed her hand to his chest and snuggled against him. Before he knew it, she was asleep.

Darien had no idea how soon his suggestion would be tested, but two days later he found himself with a packed duffel bag sitting next to Safire on the Tri-Rail bound for the West Palm Beach station. He had gotten a call earlier that morning.

"Hey, Darien. I have a proposition for you. I missed my cruise last year because one of my bosses went into labor. So I started planning this trip to Palm Beach with a girlfriend of mine. She's ditching. You up for it? Monday's Labor Day. Palm Beach is less than two hours away. The hotel is booked. It's just for the weekend. I'd love to spend the time with you. What do you think?"

"Slow down. What?"

"Come with me. We can leave whenever you get off work, and you can bring your schoolwork with you."

"I'm not packed. I—"

"Throw some clothes in a bag and come on!"

Darien had laughed.

"Wait," he'd said. "Let me think. I get out today at six.

And Monday is a holiday. Are we driving or taking the train?"

"Either one. You'll only need some clothes and your books. Oh, and don't forget your swimsuit. I get to see your sexy body on the beach!" she'd said and laughed out loud.

The exuberance in her voice had swayed him.

"I can get some reading done on the train," Darien had said. "What time are you done this evening?"

"I'm out at four, maybe earlier," Safire had answered.

"Let me see if I can get someone to cover my class at the Heritage Center, and you check the train schedule?"

He'd made a call and she'd gotten online. When Darien had made arrangements for his class, he called Safire back.

"Hey, Darien. There's a train just before five, six, seven—"

"Give me your new address. I'll pick you up at five."

"I'm in the same building, just a different apartment number. Call me when you're almost there."

"Will do."

Darien had gotten through his classes that afternoon, situated his art class at the Heritage Center and left the kids in the care of one of the other teachers. He'd hurried home to pack, stopped at the bank to get some cash and picked up Safire just after five. She was ready and waiting.

They held hands on the train, and she looked over her application materials while he read for one of his classes. By sunset they were checking in to their hotel room at the Four Seasons Resort Palm Beach. It was a luxurious hotel right on the beach on South Ocean Boulevard, and they had a room with two full beds. They ate at the Ocean Bistro, collected brochures to decide what to do the next day and opted that night to take a romantic stroll along the Palm Beach Lake Trail. It was beautiful being next to the water and seeing the gorgeous homes, but for Darien, it was even better being next to Safire and having his arm around her.

At around midnight, they got back to their room. Darien decided to get a little more reading done while Safire looked at the brochures and planned their weekend. When she stopped and gave him that sexy-Safire look, the one with the Cheshire cat grin, he put up his palms.

"Hey, we agreed to get to know one another at another angle. Remember?"

Safire looked puzzled but seemed to let it go. Then she changed for bed, and when Darien saw her in her little silky nightgown with one-inch slip-on sandals, he nearly went back on his word.

Darien read until his body had calmed down and until Safire had gone to sleep. Then he got on top of her covers and wrapped his arms around her to hold her as they slept without risking temptation. He was tempted anyway. But more, he wanted to know this woman, really know her. She had begun to lay claim to his heart.

Chapter 7

Safire woke up first. She found that Darien's arms were still around her, as they had been all night. He was still dressed and was sleeping on top of the covers, his long braids fanning out behind his head. She had felt so peaceful, so safe, with those arms wrapped around her all night.

She was also a little randy. She hadn't gotten any the night before, when Darien had stayed up reading, talking about them getting to know each other at another angle. That was Darien being a stick-in-the-mud, but Safire wouldn't be having that for long. Not on her vacation.

She kissed him awake, feeling down his chest to his nether region. He smiled beneath her kiss, and when she squeezed him, his body reacted. That's when he opened his eyes and sat up, still smiling. He leaned down and kissed her, but he didn't let her capture his head. He slipped through the ring of her arms and stood, stretching.

"So what do you have planned for us today?" Darien asked.

Safire pouted and threw the covers off, feeling her breast with one hand and her thigh with the other. "Forget what I planned. Come to me."

Darien's jaw dropped, and a bashful smile played over his face. He stood looking at her for a long time. Then he finally sat down on the bed facing her. Next, however, he proceeded to tickle her until she squealed and sprang the other way, scooting off the bed.

"Aha," he said. "You're ticklish."

"Yes, and I'm going to change before you make me pee myself."

Darien laughed, and Safire, temporarily thwarted, went into the bathroom to shower. She came out with a towel around her to get dressed, and Darien went into the bathroom to shower. Safire put on a short, yellow sundress and yellow gladiator sandals with two-inch heels, and when Darien came out of the bathroom, he was wearing a pair of blue jeans with a long-sleeved, white T-shirt and a beige vest that had a block embroidery pattern in blue.

After breakfast in the hotel, they took a tour of Palm Beach and West Palm Beach. In two hours, they got off the bus in West Palm Beach and made their way to the Norton Museum of Art, which housed a huge collection with over seven thousand pieces of art. They didn't take a tour, but they wandered the exhibit for almost three hours, talking about the art.

"Do you like stuff like this," Darien asked, "or did you pick this for me?"

Safire smiled and squeezed his arm. They'd been linked hand in hand since the bus tour. "Both," she answered. "And I knew that you'd be able to tell me all kinds of things about the art."

"The collections they have here are awesome. The photographs—"

"Let's go to the museum store before we leave."

They did, and they both got postcards as keepsakes; they didn't want to carry anything heavier because Safire had other plans for them. It was the middle of the afternoon by the time they were done, and they caught a cab to Clematis Street, where they had a late lunch and toured the shopping district. There were water fountains, and also a marketplace with kiosks. Arts-and-crafts vendors sold their wares, and as the sun began to set, the outdoor concerts started. Safire had a great time with Darien while they wandered the streets, stopping to window-shop, pausing to listen to music, lingering with ice cream near one of the fountains. Before they realized it, several hours has passed. They split a salad for dinner and went to a pub for dessert.

Then, following Safire's plan for their day, they picked a club and went dancing. Safire could tell that Darien was a bit rusty at first, but the club was so crowded that it didn't matter what you did, and soon they were both having a good time. Now this felt like a vacation.

The place was called the Grotto, and the music on the main dance floor was fast, but after an hour, the pair wandered upstairs and found another bar and another dance floor. Here the music was slower. Safire put her arms around Darien, and they held each other close and moved to the music. The heat began to rise between them as their bodies touched. Safire caressed Darien's neck with her fingers until he was excited against her, and then she pressed herself to that place until she was wet and intoxicated with desire. Now, this was more like it.

After Safire finished her second drink, they took a cab back to the hotel. During the ride, Darien put his arm around her. Safire put her head on his shoulder and took hold of his other hand. She closed her eyes and felt at ease. Being with Darien made everything more special, more exciting. She couldn't wait to make love to this man.

When they got to their room, Safire pulled out her sexiest nightgown and her slip-ons with the one-inch heels and took her toiletry bag into the bathroom to change. Her nightgown was a lilac baby-doll set made out of lace with satin panels. It was cut close to the bust and flared a bit at the hip. It barely covered her upper thigh and had a matching thong. Safire put that on, touched up her makeup, put up her hair and stepped into her slippers. She opened the door to the bathroom and stood there, looking at Darien and hoping he could read her desire.

Darien certainly noticed her. His eyes glazed over for a moment, but then he seemed to come back to himself. He was at the table in their room with one of his schoolbooks. He didn't move.

"You look incredibly beautiful, Safire."

She smiled and twirled for him, lifting up her gown as she did. "I was hoping you would notice."

He shook his head. His eyes were glued to her, but he also seemed resigned. He sighed and then said, "I thought we agreed to get to know one another without the physical for a while."

"No, you suggested it, and I disagreed. I don't think it has to be one or the other."

"Just for a little while. Just until I know more about you and know…"

Safire went to him, moved his book and sat on his lap. "Know what? What do you need to know?"

"I want to know that you're serious about me."

"I've never liked anyone like this," Safire said. It felt like a confession because she meant it; she hadn't felt like this for anyone. "I want to see where it goes. But while we're seeing that, why can't we be together?"

Before he could answer, Safire kissed his lips, and soon she had closed her eyes and was lost in the moment. Darien cupped her hips and put her from his lap.

"Slow down, Safire. It's not going to happen. I have reading to do, and we need to spend some time outside the sheets getting to know one another."

Safire had never been put off by a man before. It infuriated and embarrassed her. She turned on her heel and walked to her bed filled with righteous fury.

"Since when did you turn into a priest?"

"I'm not a—"

"Then who put you in charge? Who made you the sex police? Saying when we do and when we don't and—"

"I thought we agreed to get to the platonic stage—working in the inverse."

"I didn't agree to that. That's not me."

"No, and you haven't kept anyone you've caught. You've thrown them all back. Why is that? Maybe what happens between the sheets isn't enough. Maybe I want more than that."

Maybe, thought Safire, this isn't meant to be. Mr. Rogers from *Mister Rogers' Neighborhood* did not make a suitable companion for her. She had already gotten under the covers and turned away, and she refused to listen further. She sure as hell didn't need a Clark Kent when she could have a Superman. And she understood that he wanted to take things slowly. That just wasn't her way. She'd gotten a series of red signals on the first night they went to the sports bar, so she couldn't claim to be surprised. He was a veggie-eating, nondrinking, nonpartying stick-in-the-mud. He hadn't misrepresented himself. When it was all said and done, they were simply too different.

The more Safire thought about it, the more this seemed to be true. And it was better to face the fact now that they were not on the same channel and never would be. She was *Sultry after Sunset,* and he was *Country Now* or *The Hallelujah Choir.* And for him to push her away like that. She'd never had anyone make her feel like that just because she was in control of her sexuality and chose when to use it. Oh, hell, no. Safire didn't go down like this.

That was it. She'd play it cool until Monday, when they got back to Miami, and then she would phase him out of her life altogether.

Angry as she was, this thought didn't relieve her of tension. It just made Safire suddenly sad. She had felt differently about Darien. It had felt special. She wasn't sure how or why, just that it did. Now that was gone. There was an empty space where there had been…something. Perhaps the promise of love.

Safire had spent so much energy trying to make it on her own that she hadn't really factored in love. There was always the possibility that things might click with one of her beaus, but it was only that—a potentiality. She never needed it to become real. She was always focused on having a life, being independent, doing it on her own. She never had anyone who competed with that goal—not until Darien.

And it didn't make sense, as different as they were. Why would he be the one to make her feel things she wasn't used to feeling? Maybe she was just ready to have a relationship, and he was there at the right time. But with school coming up, that didn't make sense either. No, it was something about him, something about the way he touched her chin… and touched her spirit.

Well, that hadn't lasted long. The differences between them would always end up overshadowing the attraction between them. And Safire wasn't going to be pushed away again. No. Hell, no. Darien was right about one thing; she was used to getting what she wanted when it came to dating a man. And she had no reason to put up with anyone who offered less.

It was a while before Safire fell asleep. Luckily, Darien stayed awake longer, and nothing more was said that night.

Safire awoke alone. Darien was still at the table and still in the same clothes. His bed hadn't been slept in, and he had schoolwork spread across the tabletop. Safire got up, gathered her things and went into the bathroom. She had no desire to be seen by Darien again until she was dressed. While she showered, she tried to figure out a way to make the best of it. She might as well enjoy as much as she could of her vacation. She would be pleasant, but that was it.

Only that wasn't it.

When Safire came out of the bathroom, she found that Darien had cleared the table and gathered his things to shower.

"The bathroom's open," she said.

"Safire, can we talk for a moment?"

"I don't think we need to do that. I know where you stand. You know where I stand. We just don't agree."

"We do need to talk," he said. "Please, come and sit with me."

Safire sighed and walked toward the table. Before she could claim a chair, however, Darien had scooped her onto his lap and held her lightly against his chest. She didn't face him, but he kissed the back of her head. She still didn't turn around. He was acting as if nothing had happened. Well, nothing had happened. That was the problem.

"Safire, about last night, I pushed you away, and I think that might have hurt you. I'm sorry. I never want to hurt you. I just wanted to slow things down a little bit. I know I'm a hypocrite for wanting to since I haven't been able to keep myself from being with you, but just for a little I wanted to slow down, to know you in a different way. I guess because you tell me so little, I worry that all it is to you is physical or that I'll be one of the ones that you throw back. Look, from now on we talk things out, and we both decide. Only, we keep the other's feelings in mind, and we decide for us."

Safire hated that Darien was being so sweet and confusing things that she had clear in her mind. There was something winning about that sweetness, and part of her wanted to give in to it.

He wrapped his arms around her. "You don't know how hard it was for me last night to keep from making love to you. You're so beautiful, and last night you were so incredibly sexy. And I don't think women are tramps or that you are because you have needs or because you want me. I'm sorry if I sent the wrong message when all I meant to do was slow things down. How about if before tonight, we talk things through?"

On the one hand, Darien was saying all the right things, but on the other, he still wanted to go slowly, which frustrated Safire. How could it work between them? They were still just too different.

That much decided, Safire nodded curtly, got off Darien's lap and decided to pursue her plan to make the most of the day. The problem was that the day went wonderfully, confounding her determination.

After Darien dressed, they had breakfast and went into West Palm Beach to visit the Palm Beach Zoo.

Darien looked at the monkeys and then back at Safire. There was a quizzical look on his face. "And you picked a zoo because...?"

Safire swatted him and couldn't help seeing the humor in her choice. "I know someone I might want to bring here. I wanted to check it out. My first choice was McCarthy's Wildlife Sanctuary, but they require reservations."

"So you like animals?" he asked.

"Some," she answered. "The peacocks are beautiful."

"That they are."

Darien kept his palm at her back or his arm around her. Safire didn't encourage it; she just wanted to make it through the day. But she was surprised to find herself laughing with Darien, getting along. They strolled the zoo and took in the tigers, the alligators, the pelicans. They even started talking again, a little about his art, a little about her working with children, a little about her paralegal work.

When they had tired of the zoo, they took a cab to City-Place. They walked and window-shopped a bit to take in the feel of the European-style town, and then they found a restaurant for lunch. While they were eating, Darien got

Safire talking and laughing about some of the people she'd dated, and she got him to open up a bit more about his days playing the field. She couldn't really imagine it, given his newfound moderation, except that he looked so good that it was, after all, easy to picture.

The rest of the day was for the beach. Safire changed out of her clothes, tied on her bikini, threw on a sarong and a cover-up and her slip-on sandals and grabbed her towel. Darien was ready before she got out of the bathroom, having put on his trunks and replaced his jeans. He grabbed his towel and they were off.

Safire had brought the sunblock and was getting along well enough with Darien to leave her aloofness aside and let them lotion each other's backs. It was over eighty degrees, and the water was wonderful. They played for a little while, swam and then played some more. Safire had packed two blow-up floaters and a ball.

"How did you get all this into your suitcase?" Darien asked.

"My clothes are small, and my nightclothes don't take up any space at all," she said and chuckled, surprised that she could make fun about it. "Actually, neither does my swimsuit."

Darien looked at her in her little bikini, and Safire thought she saw a glimmer of lust in his eyes. "It suits you beautifully."

"Your trunks suit you just, as well. You have large, gorgeous thighs."

Darien reddened a bit but smiled. "Thank you."

When they got the floaters blown up, they drew them into the water and lolled for a while.

"Next time," Safire said, "we go out with the scuba-diving group."

"I'm game."

"Me, too. We have to do this again tomorrow."

"Then we will."

Back onshore, they added some more lotion and tanned. As the sun started to set, they took their last long swim and then packed up.

Safire hit the shower first. She got off the sand, pulled back her wet hair and put on some makeup. She wore a little powder-blue dress with silver at the hem and waist, and she came into the room to put on her strappy silver heels and spray on perfume. She was ready for dinner.

When Darien came out of the bathroom, Safire had her feet up on a chair and was leafing through one of his schoolbooks. He wore a pair of purple jeans but hadn't put on his shirt as yet. Safire looked briefly at his hard, naked chest and turned back to the book. Darien put on his shirt and shoes and stood watching her.

Safire glanced up to see if Darien was ready to go, and she saw an expression of raw desire in his eyes that made her hold her breath. She still wanted this man. She stood up as he stepped toward her, and she was about to put her arms around him and kiss him when she remembered last night. She stopped and turned away.

Darien caught her and drew near to her. "Don't ever decide not to kiss me, Safire. I'll never push you away again, whether or not we—"

Her lips cut off his words, and their arms encircled one another. Their kisses were hard and thirsty and needy. They had been parched for each other, teased by each other, for so long. Safire felt consumed by the masculinity of this man—his hard arms, his firm grip, his heady scent. She moved her hands between them to feel the contours of his chest. She didn't know if he would stop them, only that her whole body craved the taste and touch of this man.

He brought one of his hands to her chest and stroked her nipples into peaks through the thin cotton of her dress. Her chest heaved toward him, and she murmured. His hand returned around her. When he unzipped her dress and slipped his hands inside to run them along her back, she knew that they would make love. This knowledge sent a shudder through her middle and freed her to seek him.

Safire unbuckled Darien's belt and pulled at his jeans, freeing him. When her hand found him, his hips tilted toward her, and he groaned. She slipped to her knees, taking him into her mouth and licking the rich, dark chocolate of his skin. He bucked and pulled her upward—too sensitive or too ready.

Their mouths found each other again, just as hungry as before. Darien cupped her rear and raised her against his leaping core. Safire felt a sweet ache and began to throb at her center. He made her so ravenous, so eager, as no one else ever had.

He lifted her and spilled her onto the bed, where he tugged her panties off, spreading her before him. Darien's body dipped down, and his mouth covered her. He sucked in her tender crown, making her body arch off the mattress. He ran his fingers over her wetness, making her fists ball. She pushed his head back, not wanting it to end so soon.

Darien stood and began taking off his clothes. Safire shimmied out of her dress and then undid her bra, dropping her clothes next to the bed. She motioned for her purse so that she could rummage for a condom. When she found one, she opened it and rolled it onto his flicking limb.

As Darien climbed onto the bed and lowered himself over her, Safire leaned up, touching his face as it moved toward her. Despite their passion, despite their yearning, a softness also sprang up between them. Darien's hand riffled through Safire's hair. He cupped her head as she raised it, and they kissed with a gentle urgency. It had never been like this for her before.

When Safire lowered her head back down and opened her eyes, Darien was leaning on his elbows, smiling at her.

She couldn't help smiling back. He brought one hand between them and pressed her nipple between his fingers. Then he watched her as her body flailed in response. He moved his hand farther down and kneaded her sex with his thumb, watching as she winced and tossed.

"You're so beautiful, Safire," he said.

Safire wrapped her legs around Darien's waist and brought him toward her. He replaced his arm at her side and let her guide him. God, how she wanted this man.

When his thick member hit her drenched shores, her entire body contracted, and a delicious agony gripped her.

"Yes, Darien, please."

A guttural sound issued from Darien's throat, and then he filled her. He laid claim to her lips with his own and began to toil. Safire clenched and cried out as he began churning inside her, raking his chest over her breasts. He reached down between them again and covered her inflamed crest with his fingers. Safire cried out once more, dancing along his swollen trunk, as the exquisite anguish overtook her senses. She trembled and clung to his arousal as she thrust. A sensuous convulsion burst throughout her body, and she was catapulted over the threshold of her own pleasure. Darien spun inside her momentarily, then bucked and went taut, joining her abandon.

Darien turned them on the bed to hold her, and Safire folded herself into his arms. It was never like this with anyone else.

After they had calmed and kissed and cooled, Darien tweaked her nose.

"So much for slowing things down," he said.

"I know," Safire responded. "We didn't talk either. Do you mind terribly?"

"No, I don't. You're hard to resist."

Safire smiled at that. She laid her head on his chest, and he strummed his fingers through her hair.

They ordered room service and spent the night in, watching a movie and holding each other until they fell asleep.

The next morning, they made love again, and then they hit the beach for the last time. They showered and checked out, leaving their bags at the hotel. They had several hours before having to catch the train, so they took a ferry ride out to the Palm Beach Maritime Museum. Safire wasn't as into such things as her sister, who was a historian, but she and Darien enjoyed the exhibits and displays and each other.

They got back in time to have lunch, collect their bags and make it to their Tri-Rail train. There was a closeness between them now. Darien read on the trip to get ready for classes the next day, but he kept Safire's hand in his, and he looked up periodically to smile at her. Safire was happy with their new bond. She liked having her hand in his and always looked up from her novel in time to smile back at him. She was still not sure that they weren't too different, but she was starting to think that Darien James might be worth slowing down for.

Chapter 8

Darien closed his book for Critical Studies in the Visual Arts and stretched. His teacher had just finished wrapping up, and the class was dispersing. He needed to do research for his final paper for this class and had already requested some books on interlibrary loan, so his next stop was the library. Darien wanted to advance studies on the iconography of Harlem Renaissance art, but he needed to select his artists, narrow his topic and do the necessary research. He also had to meet Safire at her place in a few hours, so he needed to get a move on. He did what he could in the library, collected the books that he'd ordered and went home to change.

He had been out with Safire several times in the past few weeks—since their trip to Palm Beach. They were getting to be a regular item. Yet he wasn't sure where he stood with her. She seemed to enjoy their time together, and she seemed to love their physical intimacy, but she still didn't let him into her private mind very much. She held him outside of her deep-down thoughts and emotions.

If he didn't already have feelings for her, it wouldn't matter. But he did. He was starting to fall for her. The time they spent together and the love that they made only intensified his feelings. He worried that he might be one of the ones she tossed back. Was it more physical than emotional for her? He didn't know how she felt. Well, tonight he would ask her. If wanting someone who had real feelings for him chased her away, that would be as telling as anything she could say.

Darien pulled on a pair of blue jeans and picked out a multicolored patchwork shirt from his closet. He stepped into his black penny loafers and added a dab of cologne. Then he pulled a leather strap with inlaid African bone over his head and took his braids out from under it. He was ready to go.

When he arrived at Safire's place, he parked next to her car and headed toward her building. As he approached her door, he saw Safire. At first she seemed to be talking to another man, a shady-looking one. But as he peered farther, he saw the man grab Safire's purse and put it over his shoulder. Darien started running toward them. The man had grabbed Safire by the shoulders and was trying to force her backward toward the door. Safire kicked him in the shin, and he hopped back a step on the other leg. Then Darien was upon them.

At running speed, Darien rammed the other guy, who flew into the air and landed on his side. The man was a bit bigger than Darien, but Darien had the force of conviction. When the guy sprang up, Darien tackled him back down, landing on top of him with a punch to his stomach. The man doubled over on his side.

As Darien got up, he ripped Safire's purse from the guy's shoulder and handed it to her.

"I'll go get the security guard," Safire said and ran into the building.

Darien was still standing over the man when Safire came back with the guard, who was on a walkie-talkie calling another guard in the building. The two guards detained the man until the police arrived to take statements from them and take the assailant into custody.

Their night, which was to have been a late movie and dinner, had been thrown off course. Safire had been running late to begin with. Now, neither of them felt like it, and they couldn't have made the movie anyway. They went up to Safire's, both frazzled and uptight.

Safire brought Darien some lemonade and poured herself a glass of red wine, and then they settled for a few moments on the couch, Darien's arm anchored protectively around Safire's shoulder.

"I don't know what I would have done if anything had happened to you, Safire," he said and then kissed her temple.

"I'm okay, just a bit unsettled."

Darien shook his head and sighed. He repositioned himself, taking Safire's hand, and turned to her.

"Safire, I know you won't want to hear this, but I have to say it. And I'm not blaming the victim or saying that it wouldn't have happened anyway."

"What are you saying?" she asked.

"He had your purse, and he didn't run with it. He didn't just want your money. He wanted you."

"So he's a lecher and a rapist."

"Safire, maybe you should dress a bit more conservatively."

"Are you kidding me?" she asked, getting an attitude.

Darien tried to stay calm. "No, I'm not."

Safire jerked her hand from his. "You *must* be kidding. I didn't even get a chance to change into my come-hither clothes, and you're thinking it's the way I'm dressed? Oh, hell, no."

"Wait. Look at what you have on."

Safire had on her usual skirt suit. This one was a goldenrod color with a camisole to match. The skirt had a slit in the back, and as usual, it was cut well above her knee. This one had a one-inch sheer ruffle around the bottom of the skirt and around the bottom hem and cuffs of the jacket, which had a deep V-neck. She had on her two-and-a-half-inch black pumps, and her hair was loose.

Safire was on her feet, clearly fuming.

"You're telling me what not to wear? Do I tell you not to sculpt nudes?"

"That's not the same, now, is it?"

"I wore this in court today, Darien." She was pacing like a caged ferret. "The judge didn't seem to think I look like I'm a whore. Maybe that's what's on *your* mind—for all your innocent act. I—"

"On anyone else it would just be a suit, Safire. But on you," Darien said, standing and taking Safire's face between his palms, "it's devastating."

Safire was quiet for a moment, but the battle wasn't over.

"I don't want to snuff out your light or tame you. I just want you to be careful. What if I hadn't been there? What if—"

"You mean, what if some man wasn't standing about so he could rescue me? I seem to do pretty well on my own and—"

"You don't have to do it on your own," Darien said softly.

That stopped Safire for a moment but only a moment. She stepped away from him and shook her head.

"No. I won't go about trying to look frumpy because there are predators in this world. I won't let who I am get taken from me because there are those who can't keep their hands to themselves." She shook her head. "And just so you know, dress and attractiveness have little significance in rape. Studies reveal that all kinds of women are targeted, regardless of behavior or dress or age. Go online and see for yourself. Get better informed."

"Okay, so I stand corrected, but it can't hurt to tone it down just a little."

"You just missed my point, Darien. I think the problem is that *you* are conservative, and you want me to be like you."

"I may be conservative in some ways, but you are… unrestrained in other ways."

"So maybe this can't work," Safire said and shrugged, looking down at the coffee table.

"Why can't we meet in the middle?"

"I'm not a middle-of-the-road-type girl, Darien. I'm not going to change the way I dress."

"Okay." Darien sighed, a bit exasperated but realizing that Safire would always be Safire. "Then how about some other things? Carry Mace or pepper spray. Take a self-defense class maybe. What else?"

"I can carry Mace. A self-defense class will have to wait a bit. I like those suggestions. But I'm still concerned about your first one. It's based on a misconception, and it points to great differences between us."

"Let's table that for now. I love how beautiful you look. I'm just…worried."

"I was scared, too," Safire said.

Darien went to her and held her. All his being wanted to protect this woman. He would never let anyone harm her. That was why it scared him that she was so beautiful and that she let it show. But she was right. No amount of dressing down would hide her beauty. And maybe she was right not to let the threat of perverts rob her of her style. Still, it made his job harder.

Darien felt Safire's lips on his neck, and his whole body responded to that luscious touch. He tipped his forehead down to her and looked in her eyes. She tilted her head up to his and kissed his lips. Soon the balmy gust that had risen between them was a squall. Their kiss intensified, and Darien could feel Safire's urgency rising. Soon there would be a full-blown hurricane.

Darien broke their kiss. He'd never been inside her new place before.

"What about your roommate?" he asked.

"She's cool. She's probably asleep already. Come."

Safire took Darien's hand and led them to her room, where they made love, his worry transforming into tenderness, her fear melting into desire. It was slower and more affectionate than any of the other times they'd been together, but no less passionate, no less electric.

Afterward, they lay together, caressing one another—at least until Safire's stomach grumbled, and she got up to make them sandwiches.

They ate in her room. It was late, too late for the question he'd wanted to ask, the revelations he'd hoped they would share. Darien contented himself with the feel of Safire's head on his chest, the feel of his hand in her hair.

"I love making love with you. You're an amazing lover," Safire said, and Darien could tell that she was smiling as she tapped his chest with her fingernails.

It was a compliment, but it worried him. That wasn't all he wanted her to love.

"I try," he mustered. "You don't have to try."

She smiled again at that. He was falling in love with his smiling Cheshire cat. She was bullheaded and beautiful and rambunctious, and she was affectionate when she let herself be, when her guard was down. He hadn't found out what had put her guard up, but he knew that at least part of the reason was the loss of her parents. He wanted to know more. And maybe that was the greatest lure on his heart—her layers. She was a piece of crimson agate with a sharp, crystalline exterior and an array of ruby strata and a beating red heart.

Darien fell asleep with his arms around Safire and woke up to an empty bed. He heard the shower running in her bathroom, threw on his clothes and headed toward the kitchen to see if there was anything he could use to make them breakfast.

In the dining room he ran into Safire's roommate. She had on a modest pair of floral pajamas and a thick yellow robe. Her hair was back in a ponytail, and she had on glasses that made her look a little like a schoolmarm. She matched the touches about the apartment that he could tell were hers—the doilies on the end tables, and the teddy bears in the corner of the living room, the plastic flowers in the dining room—all the girlie and matronly stuff that clashed with Safire's sleek, modern look.

"So you're Safire's new boy toy. You *are* a hottie. It's nice to meet you. I'm Janelle Hawkins."

Darien hadn't liked what she'd said, but he didn't let it show. "Hi," he responded. "I hope it's okay if I'm here. Will I be in your way if I rummage in the kitchen for a few minutes?"

"No, help yourself."

Darien went into the kitchen and looked in the fridge. Was he a boy toy to Safire? Had she described him that way?

There were eggs, so he started breakfast. He knew Safire used the word *hottie* a lot, but that was another thing, unless it was paired with *boy toy*. Last night she hadn't said that she loved him. She'd said that she loved making love with him. Darien shook his head. The puzzle pieces were filling in a rather unbecoming picture.

Darien looked at the eggs, remembered the roommate—Janelle—and went back into the dining room.

"Would you like some eggs?"

"None for me. But thanks."

"Okay."

He wanted to ask her about the boy-toy comment, but he didn't know how to word that question, not without giving away his concern—and his embarrassment. He looked down. His shirt was open. He closed it.

Darien covered the eggs and readied the bread in the toaster. Janelle probably didn't even fully understand what she had said. If Safire thought he was a boy toy, he would have to show her that he could be more, that they could have more. He sensed in everything that they did together they could have something real. He would have to show her that their relationship could be more than just physical.

He popped down the toaster. He was ready to do and be more.

Chapter 9

Safire closed her book. This was going to be one of the busiest Sundays of her year, and she had gotten up early to spend some time getting ready for her reading groups. The younger class was reading an illustrated book of poems by Maya Angelou. The older class had begun evolving into a literature-and-film class. This week they were reading an excerpt of *The Autobiography of Malcolm X* and watching clips from Spike Lee's movie. Next week was Alice Walker's *The Color Purple*.

It was only nine o'clock, but Safire had engagements all day. First it was brunch with some of her girls. She'd been ditching them because of her work at the Heritage Center and in order to help more with her little brother and so that she could spend some of her free time with Darien. Today, they were meeting at Moody's at ten.

When Safire got there—late—her girls were already there. They chided her for being absent from their happenings, ribbed her over the new man in her life and resituated her within their fold. Mostly, they wanted to hear about the new man.

"Give up the goods, sugar," Rayelle said. "Tell us about the new man."

"Uh-huh," Jackie echoed. "Who's been keeping you

away from us? He must be one fine hunk of burning love to have you occupied this long."

"Hottie. She called him a hottie," Camilla said. "And does he taste as good as he looks? You were trying to find out."

"And you know," Amelia said, "she took him to Palm Beach when I couldn't go."

"Get out of here. How long have you known this man?" Unique asked.

"Apparently, long enough," Rayelle said.

Her girls raised their hands and snapped.

"You all are too much for me," Latoya said. "We need mimosas."

"Tell us *something*," Jackie demanded.

"Okay, okay," Safire said. "He's an artist, and he's an Adonis."

She realized that she was giving her girls an empty sketch to shut them up. She didn't want to reveal how much she liked Darien, how amazing it was—in the bedroom and out. She didn't want to say something that might not come true. She also was a private person, to some extent. And it occurred to her that this was even true with Darien. She might need to work on that.

But there was a bit more to it. Individually, she could confide in her girls, but as a group, they would end up teasing her to no end—at least at first. Putting that together with how tight-lipped she was in the first place, and she surely wouldn't say anything now, at least not yet, not before she had a permanent, full-fledged reason to withstand their ribbing. As always, Safire didn't want to reveal herself, but now she actually had something to reveal. She was dating someone—for real. She'd dated a lot, but not like this. She played it off, or tried to.

"I've seen him a few times," she added, "but I have to see where it goes."

"Where it goes?" Camilla eyed her. "That's a little new."

"Now, leave sweet pea alone," said Latoya. "She's always open to possibility." Latoya turned to look for the waiter. "Now, where are the mimosas?"

Luckily, they had a lot of catching up to do, so they didn't focus on Safire for too long. And actually, Safire had to be the first to leave. She was meeting her sister across town to look at more wedding dresses and to shop for cocktail dresses and lingerie for Angelina's honeymoon.

They were starting at the bridal store, and Safire got there in time to see her sister going inside. Safire greeted Angelina with a hug and a smile and then watched while Angelina tried on a series of gowns. Safire always liked the strapless ones that hugged the body down to the hips or thighs. She thought they accented all of her sister's curves. As usual, though, Angelina wanted something more traditional. Today, Angelina's favorite was a sleeveless gown with an open back that hugged her body down to the thighs but then flared out in back. This was Safire's top choice, too, and they were both leaning toward it.

Safire couldn't help envying her sister a little bit. She wanted Angelina to have the whole world laid at her feet for all that she'd been through raising their little brother and looking after their great-aunt and cousin, but she also couldn't help thinking of Darien and wondering what it would be like to shop for a wedding dress of her own.

"If you get that dress," she said to Angelina, "save it for me. I might want to use it someday."

Her sister's eyes opened wide, and her mouth gaped. Then she got a quizzical look on her face.

"This new guy has had an impact, hasn't he?"

"Maybe, we'll see."

But Safire couldn't help smiling.

The next stop was lingerie. Here was where her sister needed her advice the most. Angelina seemed hesitant to even go into the store. Safire took her older sister's arm, and the two went through the door hand in hand, like conspirators. Safire had a blast picking things out for Angelina to try.

"Don't think about me, Angelina. Think about the way Jeremy will look when he sees you. Come on. He's a good guy. He deserves it."

Whenever her sister hedged, Safire gave her a pep talk and asked, "Does it fit?" If it did, it went in the basket—all except the red number with bows.

They had more of a chance to talk looking for cocktail dresses.

"I have specific directions from Jeremy on this, Angelina. He likes what you wore on the cruise, and those were mine, so go with me here."

"These are so expensive."

Safire put an arm on her sister's shoulder. "You're marrying a doctor, and you also have your own income. Get over it. You deserve it."

"I know," Angelina said, ever cautious, "but we have Philly and Alex and a new house."

"You'll be renting the old one, so you'll have income from that. And by the time Philly goes to college, we'll both be able to help him."

Angelina held up their last selection, a maroon off-the-shoulder gown. "But they don't all have to be thigh-high."

"Okay, not all," Safire said, "just ninety percent. Remember, he liked mine. And next time we go shopping, we're going to get you some proper heels."

"No deal. I can't walk in those things you wear."

"I'll show you ones you can."

"Speaking of men," Angelina said, obviously being careful about the topic she was about to broach, "how are things going with your new flame? Are you still seeing a lot of him?"

"All there is to see." Safire winked at her sister.

Angelina gawked, and Safire broke out laughing. She loved scandalizing her sister, and it took so little.

"Actually," Safire admitted, "I like him a lot, maybe more. But we're also really different. I don't know. But being around him is…exhilarating." Safire knew she was gushing a bit, but this was her sister, so she didn't worry as much.

"Aw…" Angelina touched her cheek. "You really do like him, don't you?"

"Yeah."

"Well, when do we get to meet him?"

"Maybe tonight, if he can come. I haven't told him about it yet. I've been so busy. Oh, no," Safire looked at her watch. "I'm supposed to meet him at five. I have to run. Let's get these rung up."

The sisters hugged at the door, and Safire ran to her car. She was meeting Darien outside a place called Intimate Encounters, a place that would just shock her sister. And that was the point. Safire was going to get her present for Angelina's bachelorette party, and she wanted something outrageous. She'd done the sentimental thing for the wedding—engraved wineglasses and a family album and all of that. She wanted the bachelorette party to be scandalous.

Safire checked her face in the rearview mirror and smoothed down her skirt. She had worn a little black skirt with a ruffled hem. It was chiffon, but it was lined, and it hit her well above the knee. She had a white top that had ruffles hanging down from a low V-neck and from the cuffs. She tied these together with a wide black belt and her black pumps.

She was a few minutes late, and Darien was waiting for her outside the store. Darien had on blue slacks and a blue-and-purple shirt, and he looked as handsome as always, with his muscular shoulders showing beneath his shirt and his diamond-cut features smiling. One of his braids hung down from his temple. She tweaked it when she was close enough, and then she greeted him with a kiss and a smile.

"We can't have eye candy like you standing outside a store like this. Some randy woman might get ideas and try to carry you off," she said, and then laughed.

"Have you ever been in this store before?" Darien asked. He evidently had not.

"I most certainly have," Safire replied, taking his arm the way she had taken her sister's arm. "Come along."

Darien watched Safire as she perused the store's supply of sexual paraphernalia, hanging back a little from the counters and the clothing racks.

Safire tickled his side and whispered, "If you see anything for us, just let me know." He smiled but didn't say anything.

Finally, unable to make up her mind, Safire talked to the woman at the counter. "I need something that two people can use, that's electric and that's great for a bachelorette party."

They had just the thing.

"This has a long cord so either partner can operate it. It has eight speeds and can be used on either partner."

"I love it," Safire said. "Do you like it?"

Darien shrugged, noncommittal. "Will your friend like it?"

"She'll just die! But if she uses it, I think she'll love it."

"Okay," he said. "Then this is it."

To go with it, Safire picked a skimpy baby-doll nightie with a matching thong. Angelina was going to have a fit, but Jeremy was going to love it—if she could get Angelina to wear it. She held it up for Darien.

"You like?"

He shrugged and nodded.

"Do you want to pick one for me?" Safire asked him.

"Maybe one's enough for today."

After shopping, they went to a nearby Chinese restaurant where both she and Darien could find something to eat.

"Did it bother you to go in there?" Safire asked. "You were rather quiet." Safire had noticed Darien's reserve—another difference between them. She wanted to know if this would be a problem between them or if there was something else wrong. He'd been a little reserved since the last time he'd come to her apartment, and she didn't know why. Today, though, he was more reticent than he had been over their past few talks.

"No." He smiled. "I guess I'm not used to...places like Intimate Encounters." He pursed his lips, and she wondered if he was saying all that there was to be said. "I just hope," he added, "that you don't like that stuff better than the real thing."

Safire touched Darien's face. "Never with you."

Darien kissed her palm and then smiled.

"We can use playthings together sometimes if you'd like," he offered.

Safire just smiled, her mind flashing to erotic scenes between them.

"I don't have long today. I have a dinner party to go to. I was hoping you could come."

"I can't," Darien said. "I have to get ready for tomorrow. I wish I could. I'd like to meet some of the people in your life."

Safire pouted, disappointed.

"Don't worry. My people aren't all risqué like me."

He must have seen her disappointment because he reached for her hand and rubbed her fingers. "Next time."

"And I'll give you more warning."

He nodded.

Safire noticed someone watching her and turned. "Hey,

I know him," she said. "And I have to get something from him. Do you mind if I go say hello?"

"Of course not," Darien said. "I'll be here."

Safire walked over to the other table and greeted an old friend, Roger, who was sitting alone.

After a cursory hug, Roger pulled out a chair for her and Safire sat down, saying that she couldn't stay because she was on a date. She looked at Darien and waved, smiling. Roger was a paralegal in another office. He was consulting with one of her bosses on a case, and Safire needed the paperwork.

"We've made all the copies from the relevant cases," Roger said. "I'll have a courier bring them over to you tomorrow."

"That'll give me time to get the exhibits done."

Safire got up to leave, but Roger got a hold of her hand. "So when do I get to see you again?"

Safire laughed it off and then said, "I'm spoken for." She nodded her head toward Darien, who was looking at her with some displeasure written over his face. She smiled at him, glad to see that he was a little jealous over her, and turned back to Roger. "But I can set you up with one of my girls."

"As long as it's not Camilla," he said, and they laughed. Camilla had met Roger, and the two had not gotten along.

"We'll see," she said and winked at him before leaving.

"Did you get what you needed?" Darien asked.

"He's going to have a courier bring it over tomorrow."

"Oh, I didn't know it was work. I thought maybe he was an ex."

"Well, technically…" Safire winced. "It didn't last."

"He still seems interested in you."

"He did ask me out," she said. Yes, Darien was definitely jealous over her. This meant that he really was into her. The thought made Safire smile.

"I hope you told him no," Darien said.

Safire put her hands on her hips. "Now, don't be telling me who I can and can't see or how to run my life," she said. But she couldn't hold the attitude and broke down laughing. "What do you think I said?"

"I don't know what you said, but I did see him holding your hand."

"Aw, you're jealous." She smiled again.

Darien shrugged. "I just don't like what I saw."

Safire leaned over and kissed Darien on the cheek. She couldn't stop smiling; it was so sweet that he was jealous. He was a little quiet during their meal, but Safire was thinking. She was thinking back to the wedding dresses that she'd seen that afternoon with her sister and imagining again which she might choose. Would Darien go for the mermaid silhouette that she liked, or would he want something more traditional for her?

She also couldn't help wondering what Darien might look like as a groom. If all went well, she was going to invite him as her date to her sister's wedding. It was still a couple months away, but she was hoping that they would still be together.

"What are you smiling at?" Darien asked her.

"Was I smiling?" she asked. She didn't want to give away her thoughts. "I don't know." Then she changed the subject. "I wish you could come tonight."

"I'm sorry I can't."

"I know. It's okay. I understand. I just wanted to show off my hot new beau." She winked at him. "And then we might be going home together afterward." Safire smiled at Darien, but his face remained tense, his brow knitted in some private thought that Safire didn't feel she should intrude upon when they had so little time. Safire sighed and refocused, wondering again if something had been bothering Darien. But it would have to wait. "I won't get home until late, and I also have to get ready for this week."

"When is the dinner?"

Safire looked at her watch. "Oh, no. It starts at seven-thirty, and I have to get across town."

"I'm finished," Darien said, "but you haven't eaten very much."

"I know, but I get to eat again. Remember?"

Darien paid the tab and walked Safire to her car. She put her Intimate Encounters bag in the backseat and then put her arms around Darien. She pressed her body against his and kissed him deeply. She really did wish he was coming tonight.

"I'll call you about next weekend," Safire said, "if I can wait that long." She laughed.

Darien shook his head. "You are insatiable, aren't you?"

"With you I am."

He kissed her and then let her go. "Call me," he said.

Safire got in her car and pulled out. She stopped and bought some wine to bring, running about five minutes late, but that wasn't a problem. Angelina and Jeremy were entertaining some of Jeremy's friends that night. Safire got there in time to pull up behind Alistair and Reggie, whom she'd met before. They had recently adopted a little boy named Tyler and were just getting out of their car in front of the old homestead.

Safire hugged both men and tickled the little one Reggie was carrying. Tyler wanted to come to her, so she took him, and the group moved up the walkway to the house. Inside, Jeremy greeted her with a hug and introduced Safire to the rest of his friends. The first was Michelle, who'd brought a date, Aaron.

There was also a man named Myron, who barely looked up when he greeted her. Alistair told her that Myron was feeling down because his long-distance relationship with a woman he met on the cruise they took in January wasn't going well. Her name was Verniece, and she lived in South Carolina. The other member of their cruise was Rudy, who had also come alone.

Safire hugged her little brother, Philly, and said hello to her cousin, Alex, and then she went to help in the kitchen.

Angelina hugged her and then asked, "Did your friend come with you?"

Safire started layering the salad components into a big wooden bowl. "No," she said, "he couldn't make it tonight." Safire pursed her lips into a little pout.

Angelina took the lasagna out of the oven. "Aw, I'm sorry. Are things okay?"

"Yeah, he just had work to do."

"Well, you can bring him anytime. Just let me know, and I'll set an extra place."

When dinner was ready, Alex took the two little ones—Philly and Tyler—upstairs, where he would watch them for the rest of the evening. Jeremy led the rest of them into the dining room. The dinner was pleasant, except that Rudy, who was seated to Safire's left, kept hitting on her all night. Other than that, Jeremy's friends seemed genial, and they all got along well. Safire was glad to see that her sister had good people in her life through Jeremy.

In fact, by the time the night was over, they were planning another get-together, and Jeremy was talking about bringing Safire, Angelina, Philly and Alex home to Houston for Thanksgiving. He wanted them to meet his family before the wedding rush. Safire didn't know about the get-together, but she was in for the trip to Houston—that was, if she didn't have another Thanksgiving invite.

It had been a long Sunday. When Safire got home there was only time to pull out some clothes for the next day and change for the night. She got into bed and stretched. Then she wrapped her arms around herself and curled on her side, wishing that she was curling into Darien's arms.

Chapter 10

Darien got home from teaching his Saturday classes at the Heritage Center and changed out of his regular clothes. He put on some old, ratty sweats—his work clothes—and went into his studio. He had a few hours, and he had work that he had to get done today because tomorrow he and his brother were taking his mother out for her birthday.

He started on the second of four lamps—a new order—which he'd already sketched out and penciled onto the wood. After two hours, the broad strokes were done, and it was time to put down the power tools and pick up the chisels. It was also a good place to stop for the night.

He was meeting Safire for dinner at eight, and she'd already said that she was keeping him for the night. He didn't mind that she wanted to make love, but he still needed to know that it was love, not just her love for the physical. He hadn't found the right moment to bring up the issue but planned to tonight over dinner. The boy-toy comment was still on his mind, as was the way she said she loved their intimacy.

Darien had a piece he was working on for his exhibit on the other end of the table. He collected his chisels and mallet and pulled his chair around to the other end. This large piece needed detail work, including some wood burning that Darien was using to etch in a fabric pattern. After

some work with the chisels and some sanding, he broke out
his pyrography tools and heated up the wood-burning pen.
The fabric pattern would take passes with at least three different nibs, so this would take a while. He could get one
pass done tonight.

Darien thought of the girl he went out with for two years
in high school, Sienna, and the way she smiled at other
boys. He didn't think anything of it until he found out that
she'd been seeing Randy, a football player. She'd been playing the field all along, and he should have known because
they were both playing the field when they met. He couldn't
tell if Safire was still playing the field or not. He didn't like
the way she'd laughed and smiled in the restaurant with her
ex-boyfriend. Maybe it wasn't a fair comparison. Maybe.

With what time he had left, Darien turned to the Safire
piece. Capturing Safire was turning out to be far more elu-
sive than he had thought. He wasn't going to work on the
piece tonight; he didn't have enough time to really start
anything. He wanted to look at it, mull it over and make
some additions to his sketch, maybe pencil in some of the
changes. Darien still needed to know more about Safire to
get the sculpture right.

He was still waiting for her to open up to him. He could
tell that she had a hard time trusting people, so he was trying to be patient. This was more than a little ironic. They
could be as intimate physically as they wanted, but when
it came to basic stuff about their lives, he knew very little.
She was guarded.

Melanie, the woman he was engaged to after college,
had been a bit like that. Only, it wasn't so much that she
was guarded as that she didn't really care. Why open up to
someone you don't plan to keep? That's not what she wanted
him for. He didn't figure this out until the end. With Safire,
he couldn't tell. Sometimes it seemed as if she didn't want
him for more than the physical either, but at other times,

they felt like a real couple. When she touched his face and told him that she'd never like toys more than she liked him, it moved his heart—and his groin. But then, the subject was still sex—a subject with which she was comfortable.

He had said he was waiting until he found the right one—no more women who played the field, no more who just wanted to have a good time. Had he found that?

Darien patted the wood chips from his clothes, turned off the light and headed into his bedroom to shower the sawdust from his body and change. Since he was meeting Safire, he pulled out a pair of black slacks, a long-sleeved black shirt and a vest that was gold with black writing embroidered on it. He finished off with some cologne, a gold chain and his black dress shoes, and he left in time to pick up a boxed red rose and get to Safire's place a few minutes early.

He pulled in near her car and cut off his engine. He had his hand on the rose when he noticed Safire sitting on the passenger side of another car—a blue Acura. A well-dressed gentleman got out of the car and opened Safire's door. She got out with her purse and a shopping bag. She had on a slate-gray dress made out of a shiny lamé and cut high on her thigh and close to her body. The man seemed a little older but was very well put together and also good-looking. Safire and the man hugged, and it wasn't a brief embrace. It was a real hug. With his hand on the small of her back, the man walked Safire to the front door. There he bent his head down to kiss Safire on the cheek. She disappeared into the building with a smile and a wave, and he got into his car and took off.

Darien was confused. It looked as if Safire had just come from a date.

He picked up the rose, got out of his car and rang Safire's buzzer. Her roommate, Janelle, buzzed him in and opened the door for him.

"Hey. Safire's running late, she's in the shower. She'll be out in a few minutes. Can I get you anything to drink?"

"No, thanks."

"Well, I have some work to do. I'll be in my room. What's your name, by the way?"

"Darien James."

"Yes, Mr. Hottie. You guys have a good time tonight. Maybe I'll see you in the morning." She smiled and went back to her room.

Now Darien was more than confused; he was starting to get angry.

When Safire came out, she had on a new dress. It was short and sleeveless with two wide shoulder straps. It was made of a brown, knit, snake-print material, and with it she wore a wide brown belt and brown heels. Her hair was up now, and her face had been newly done. She was flushed and breathless from her rush to dress, and she smiled at him and came to kiss him.

Darien accepted Safire's kiss and handed her the boxed flower, but then he pulled her down to sit and talk.

"I was downstairs when you came in. I'd just gotten here. I saw you get out of a blue Acura. Are you seeing someone else?"

"What kind of question is that?" Safire asked, clearly getting miffed.

"I just need to know. We've never talked about what we have. I don't know how you feel. I don't know if this is exclusive for you. I need to know."

"So, how many men do you think I'm sleeping with?"

"I'm hoping that it's just me," Darien said, "but I need to hear from you what this is and whether it's exclusive."

Darien thought he was being reasonable, but Safire apparently didn't.

Safire crossed her arms. "So you think I sleep with everyone? Is that it?"

"No, but I need to know. I know you used to go out with the guy at the restaurant. And I know that someone just dropped you off who seemed very familiar with you. So I'm asking you what I mean to you and whether we have something exclusive, because that's what I want with you. You can have anyone. I want it to be me and no one else. I don't want you to keep seeing other people."

Safire stood up. "So a friend drops me off at home, and you think that means I'm sleeping with him?"

"I need to hear from you," Darien said, "so that I don't have to make assumptions."

"No, you're basically calling me a whore. That's what I'm hearing."

Darien got to his feet, as well. Safire was twisting his words but refusing to give him any direct answer to his questions. He was beginning to get frustrated. "I didn't say that. But tell me, who is he? How many 'friends' do you have? And what do and don't you do with them? I need to know."

"I shouldn't have to explain who he is, Darien. That's my point." Safire jabbed at the air with her finger, punctuating her sentence. She paced away from him and then turned back. "And I'll have as many friends as I want."

"And why did your roommate call me a boy toy? Did you use that phrase about me? Is that what I am to you? Is this about the physical to you, Safire? Tell me so that I can stop wondering. Do you have real feelings for me?"

"So now, because I like physical intimacy, that's all I like. I don't have any feelings."

"I didn't say that. But I'm asking because you haven't said anything about how you feel, and I need to know."

Safire shook her head. "First, I'm a whore. Now I'm an emotionless sex machine."

"Stop twisting my words and answer a question for once. I've asked three or four, and you just shoot back questions.

Are you still seeing other people? Are you in it for more than the physical? Do you have feelings for me?"

Safire held up her palms in front of him, and Darien took a step back.

Safire crossed her arms in front of her again and shook her head.

"No. You will not grill me because you saw someone drop me off at home. No. I will not defend myself against such absurd accusations. No. I will not have this conversation. No. You need to go."

Chapter 11

Safire tapped her foot on the floor, waiting for Darien to leave. She was fully riled, and she'd more than had enough.

For a moment, Darien didn't move. Then he took a step toward the door but turned back. "I'm not asking absurd questions. I'm asking questions that I need to know the answers to. And I'm not accusing you. I'm asking."

"No," she said. "You saw somebody drop me off, and now you think you get to tell me who I see and when. You think that because I know people other than you that I must be sleeping around."

"I didn't say that. I asked because we haven't talked about that, and I don't know what your regular thing is."

"My regular thing? Apparently, you think it's being a whore. And you think that's all I want you for. Get out, Darien. I've had enough of this." Darien stepped toward her, but Safire stepped back, as well.

"I'm not the enemy here," he said. "The problem is you not saying what you feel or what the terms are of our relationship. The problem—"

"The problem is that I need a real man, somebody who goes after what he wants, somebody who's not so insecure that me being dropped off at home by another man bends him out of shape."

"Once again, your paradigm is off. A real man is someone who wants an exclusive relationship. A real man is someone who wants to be more than a boy toy. A real man is someone who goes to the source if there's a question."

"I don't need someone who slings allegations at me, Darien. I don't want to see you anymore. Get out."

Darien turned and walked to the door. "When you want a real man, you'll know where to find me. If you want to keep playing the field, then forget it." And he was gone.

Safire marched over and slammed the door after him, even angrier because he'd gotten the last word. He'd basically called her a slut two times over, and he'd gotten to stroll out as if he was the one who was wronged.

Safire picked up the boxed rose, smacked it against the dining table on her way to the kitchen and flung it in the garbage.

She thought he was getting to know her, but he didn't know her at all. He didn't want her to be available to other men, as if she was some kind of trollop just flaunting herself all over the place. He didn't know if she had feelings for him, as if she'd been seeing him for the past two months just for the sex. That's what he thought of her. She didn't need someone like that in her life. Hell, no. That was the end of it.

Come to think of it, she could leave her volunteer work at the Heritage Center at the end of the year. And one of the other law offices doing pro bono work had a paralegal who could do more intake interviews if they needed them, but it was pretty much under control now. By the end of next summer, she would be back in school and wouldn't even have to worry about that. In fact, soon she wouldn't have to worry about seeing Darien James at all.

The next day, Safire packed her things and went over to see her sister. She wasn't supposed to babysit until Thursday night, but she had called over that morning and had gotten Jeremy, who'd said that he could use some time alone with Angelina over the weekend. Safire hadn't planned to say anything about Darien, but she wanted the comfort of her sister's voice.

Now she was heading there to have lunch with the boys so that Angelina could get some papers graded. Then she was going to stay over to help her cousin, Alex, look after Philly. Alex was about to turn twenty-one, and her younger brother was just over seven. Alex could babysit by himself, but Philly had had another seizure last week, so they all wanted to be careful. Alex didn't drive, so having Safire there with her car gave them all peace of mind.

Jeremy took them to a burger place for lunch. Safire was feeling down and just stared at the juicy piece of meat on her plate. She should have known that they were too different when she found out Darien was a vegetarian who didn't get out much.

Jeremy chatted about the wedding and honeymoon plans, and he even got Alex to talk a little bit about going to school, which was more than she could do. When Philly was done eating, he took out a little handheld video game that Angelina had gotten him, and he had Safire watch him play.

Lunch kept Safire occupied, which was what she needed. And Jeremy was such a good guy, she found herself feeling a little jealous of her sister. She hadn't felt that way before yesterday, but now she had no prospects on the horizon, and she couldn't help envying the good thing her sister had.

After lunch, Jeremy went to collect Angelina. Safire took the boys for dessert and then stopped to let them pick up a movie. Alex also wanted to browse the video games because that's what he wanted to do—design video games. She asked him if he saw anything he wanted, but as usual, he said no. Safire paid for the movie and got them some popcorn, and then they headed home.

Angelina had already started packing up the home where they grew up, so there were boxes in the corners of every room. The family photographs were gone, and so were all the knickknacks her parents kept in the living room. Her father's old vinyl records had been boxed, and so had her mother's china menagerie.

Seeing the old homestead being taken apart made Safire even more melancholy. At least they were keeping the house. After it was gutted and remodeled, which it sorely needed, Angelina and Jeremy were going to rent it out. Safire hoped that the income could put Alex and Philly through school. They wouldn't have to worry about her. At the same time, her sister probably needed some assistance with all of this, and Safire decided that she could help. She'd be talking to her sister before the week was out. In fact, she'd be back on Thursday to watch Philly again. That might be a good time.

Philly and Alex started playing a video game as soon as they got home. Safire shrugged and pulled out her paperwork. She was almost finished with her applications and financial-aid forms, and she'd be sending them in after she'd had one final look at them. Tonight she read them over for changes and then put them away. She was at the dining table in the kitchen and didn't want the boys to walk in and find her with the application forms. Then Angelina would know, and Angelina would want to help her pay for school. Her sister had enough on her plate, so that was out of the question.

Safire took a break and got the boys some ice cream. Then she pulled out books for her classes at the Heritage Center. She couldn't think of the classes without thinking about Darien, and she couldn't help it when tears stung the corners of her eyes. She wiped them away quickly, wondering what had gotten into her. She never felt this let down by the end of a relationship. But then, she didn't usually have a *real* relationship—one that she thought could be going somewhere, and that she wanted to keep.

She wondered briefly if she'd been too quick to get angry at Darien. Maybe she could see why he might worry that she was still seeing other people. Maybe she should have just told him who had dropped her off. Maybe she should be touched that he was jealous and wanted something exclusive. But this logic didn't sync well. She shouldn't have to explain who he was as if she'd been caught cheating. She needed someone who knew her better than that, someone who could tell that it meant more to her than the physical. Damn him for being so insecure. And damn him for not thinking more of her.

Safire almost called Camilla, but she didn't feel like putting her business out there to her friends. Camilla was one of her closest friends, but she had a big mouth. Maybe if her sister was home, Safire could talk to her, but she also hated burdening Angelina, who already had enough to deal with.

She sighed and decided to focus. Her older students were reading a selection of Ernest Gaines's *A Lesson Before Dying.* Next week was a selection from Toni Morrison's *Beloved,* and after that was *The Women of Brewster Place* and then *To Kill a Mockingbird.* She liked having the film clips to use, so she was keeping the film-and-literature theme going. She already had her discussion questions ready for Gaines's text, so she went over those. Tomorrow, she could select clips to show.

The younger class was always harder. This week and next week, they were reading selections from *Let It Shine: Stories of Black Women Freedom Fighters,* the award-winning book by Andrea Davis Pinkney. It had beautiful allegorical images by Stephen Alcorn, and Safire got her office to put some of them on disc for her so that she could turn them into a PowerPoint for class. Now she had to figure out how to get the students talking about them—the book and the images. She decided on some vocabulary terms—heroism, symbol, allegory—and worked on her questions for a while before deciding to call it a night.

After Philly brushed his teeth and changed, Safire checked his math homework and then read to him a little bit from one of his schoolbooks. She patted his head as he yawned, almost asleep. Then she turned out his light and cracked his door on the way out.

Since she'd been helping with him more, she'd gotten a real sense of what it meant for Angelina to be responsible for him. It meant being a real, full-time mother.

Safire collected her things and said good-night to her cousin, Alex. She'd be sleeping in her great-aunt's old room tonight, and tonight this made her sad. Her great-aunt had passed away earlier that year, but that wasn't the reason she was sad tonight. She'd stayed in Aunt Rose's room before. It was her break with Darien that was bringing her down, and she knew it.

Safire cuddled against her great-aunt's pillow and felt a tear fall. She wasn't really a crier, so this was unlike her—as unlike her as when she'd cried that first night she met Darien, and over something as ridiculous as his question about jazz. Safire squeezed the pillow. She missed her mother and her father and her great-aunt.

And she missed Darien.

Somehow this new letdown brought the old sorrows to life again. One bled into the other, and they became an overlapping series of losses.

It felt as if it would kill her when she lost her mother, when the jazz albums stopped playing on weekend mornings. Then when she lost her father, it was as if the music had gone forever. She had steeled herself against those anguishes, had used determination to handle the grief and continue. She'd regained her life, her spirit. But right now, it felt as though these had been sucked away again.

Darien had made her start hoping for something more. Now she was filled with the absence of something she hadn't fully realized was there—something real.

It was better to keep her eyes on her goals. They didn't bite you back; they didn't threaten to break you. They didn't land you in a spiral of losses.

Safire squeezed her great-aunt's pillow and then squeezed the remaining tears from her eyes. The sooner she put this behind her and stopped acting like a crybaby, the better.

Chapter 12

Darien wasn't usually at the Heritage Center on a Thursday evening unless there was extra administrative work that needed to be done. Today, several staff members had met about the upcoming fund-raiser, and since a lot needed to be sorted out, the meeting lasted all afternoon and into the evening. After-school programs were now running, and he had a message for one of the tutors, so he went upstairs to the open labs.

Along the way, he thought he heard Safire's voice. He peeked through the window of a closed classroom door, and there she was, in front of a class in her usual skirt suit. He would have died if he'd had a teacher that pretty in his day.

She was with a class of students ranging from ages eight to twelve, and she had a projector showing an image on the screen at the front of the room.

"Who wants to start reading the section on Harriet Tubman?" she asked.

Several students raised their hands.

"As we read, remember the questions I'm going to ask. What obstacles did she face, and why does she fit the definition of a hero? How does this image portray her life? These are the same questions I want you to answer next week when you bring your own hero to present to the class. Jason, would you start?"

Jason started reading, and Safire wrote relevant terms on the board.

Soon she stopped him and had another student pick up and then another.

"That's enough for now. Tell me, how does this image portray Harriet Tubman? Who can talk about the star, the railroad tracks and the tunnel, and the people on her arms?"

Hands were going up all over the room.

"Come up to the front of the room and point to the part of the picture you want to talk about, and then say what it means."

She pointed to a student, who ran up to the front and pointed to the image.

"The railroad tracks stand for the Underground Railroad," the youngster said.

"That's wonderful, Libby." Safire patted the girl's shoulder, and Libby beamed. "That's what we call a symbol—something that stands for something else. The railroad tracks stand for the Underground Railroad. Who can find a passage in the book that talks about the Underground Railroad and what it was?"

Darien turned from the class, perplexed. He knew that they'd found someone to do the children's reading classes, but he didn't know it was Safire, and she'd never mentioned it. She seemed great with the kids. She had their attention, and they appeared to adore her.

If he'd known what she was doing, he could have coordinated his art class with her. The kids could have done symbolic images of their heroes to bring next week.

He delivered the note and went back downstairs to find the director.

"How long has Safire Lewis been volunteering with the after-school book-club program?"

"Ah," Mr. Johnson said. "She started soon after she came to do the interviews for the Legal Assistance Program. She had to get fingerprinted and everything, so it took a couple of weeks, but it's been... Well, let's see."

"How come I didn't know?" Darien asked. "She's up there showing slides. I could have coordinated with her."

Mr. Johnson shifted some papers on his desk. "She wanted it kept quiet. Anyway, she's just given her notice. She'll be leaving in a few weeks—at the end of this semester. She's found someone to take—"

"Why is she leaving?"

Mr. Johnson's left brow went up into an arch. "I'm not rightly sure that she said. No, just that she was sorry to go but that her colleague would be a great replacement."

"What time is her class over? Is it one of the four-to-six classes?"

"You got it."

"Thank you," Darien said and turned from Mr. Johnson's office.

Darien suspected why she was leaving—him. And he couldn't let that happen. He hadn't meant to run her out of his life, and he sure as hell didn't mean to run her out of the Heritage Center, not when they needed good people to help staff their programs.

He had another forty-five minutes. He thought about going up to observe her class. He loved seeing her working with the little kids. But he didn't want to put her off, so he spent the time getting things together for the fundraiser. When he looked up, it was quarter after six. He gathered his things quickly, hoping that he hadn't missed her, and went out to the parking lot. The student assistants often waited with the children after class, so she might have gone already.

Darien got to the parking lot in time to see Safire pull off. He jumped into his car and began following her. He couldn't let her leave the Heritage Center because of their argument. And the truth was that he hadn't stopped thinking about her in the five days since she'd told him to get lost. These were unrelated, but both propelled him to follow her across North Miami, trying to catch up with her. She drove the way she did everything else—fast.

At first, Darien thought he was following her home, but she didn't go home. She went to a house just east of Griffing Boulevard. He had to admit that part of his mind was getting ready to get angry with her for finding someone else so quickly, if that was the case.

Safire pulled up in front of a house, and a little boy who had been playing in the front yard came running to her car. She got out of her car with a satchel and a backpack in one hand and lifted the little boy to her hip with her other hand. Darien found a space across the street and parked.

Just then, the man who had dropped her off on Saturday night came out of the house, only he was with another woman, one who resembled Safire a lot but who was a little older and little taller. These two were clearly a couple.

Darien got out of his car and walked up the front pathway to the group. The gentleman took Safire's bags and then turned to him as he approached.

"Can we help you?"

That's when Safire saw him.

"Yes, I'm here to see Safire."

"Darien," she said, "how did you find me here?"

"I've been trying to catch up with you since you left the Heritage Center. You drive like Sandra Bullock in the movie *Speed*."

The other two chuckled, but Darien didn't, and neither did Safire.

"I need to talk to you," he said.

"Is this him?" the woman asked Safire on the side, but Darien heard her.

"It was him, but—"

"Maybe you should introduce us," the gentleman suggested.

Safire sighed and rolled her eyes.

"Darien, this is my older sister, Angelina, and this is her fiancé, Jeremy Bell."

"This is your sister's fiancé, the one who dropped you off on Saturday?"

"Yes, and this one—" she tickled the tummy of the little boy she was holding "—is my little brother, Phillip. We call him Philly. And inside is our cousin, Alex."

"Well," Angelina said. "I've been wanting to meet you. Will you join us for dinner? We're having lamb. Jeremy cooked."

Darien looked at Safire, who shrugged and then said, "Okay." Then she turned to her sister. "He doesn't eat meat."

"I'm fine with sides," Darien said. "You don't have to go to any trouble for me."

Inside, Safire put her brother down and introduced Darien to Alex. Then the sisters went into the kitchen. Darien couldn't make out what they were saying.

Jeremy showed him to a seat on the couch where they could watch the younger brother and the cousin playing a video game. The boys were absorbed, so the two men could talk a bit quietly.

"So," Jeremy said, "trouble in paradise."

"Is it that obvious?" Darien asked.

"What is it?"

"I'm not sure where to start. Well, let's start with Saturday, when *you* dropped Safire off at her apartment, and she neglected to tell me who *you* were."

"I see," said Jeremy. Then he chuckled.

"Well, some things—like not saying everything that should be said—run in the Lewis family. I didn't even know that one's real name until after I tracked her sister down."

He chuckled again. "But I'll say this. The Lewis sisters are worth fighting for."

"How come their brother is so little?"

"The parents had Phillip later in life. That's how they lost their mother."

"I see. What else runs in the Lewis family?"

"Other than being hardheaded and having to do everything on their own?"

Both men chuckled.

"Been there," Darien said. "Seen that."

"Dinner's almost ready," Angelina called from the kitchen.

"You guys go wash your hands," Jeremy said to Philly and Alex.

At dinner, Darien got to meet Safire's family. It turned out that Philly was seven, that Angelina was a history teacher at Florida International University, where Darien was studying art, and that Jeremy was a radiologist at Miami Children's Hospital in South Miami.

"What about you, Alex?" Darien asked.

Alex had been quiet so far. Now that Darien had turned the spotlight on him, he could see that Alex was just generally quiet.

"I'm talking online courses in design right now, but next year, if I can get in, I want to go to the Miami International University of Art and Design to study computer animation."

"That's a wonderful plan, Alex," Angelina said, obviously hearing this for the first time.

"But it's hard to get in, and tuition is expensive. Next semester, I'm going to take some more online courses and see if I can get in. If not, I can start somewhere less expensive and transfer in, maybe."

"You have the right attitude," Jeremy said. "You'll make it. And don't worry about the money."

"We can do loans," Angelina said.

"If we need to," Jeremy added.

"And I can help," Safire said.

Darien looked at Safire. She obviously hadn't told her family about her own plans for school. Was she planning to defer to help her cousin?

"That won't be necessary," Jeremy said.

"You take care of you," Angelina added, "and let us know if you need anything."

"Speaking of which," Safire said, "I can help with the packing."

"I'm doing it a little at a time, but I'll let you know when."

"Okay."

"Me, too," Philly said. "I can put stuff in boxes."

Safire was sitting next to her little brother and petted his head. "It's a deal. No more packing by yourself, Angelina."

"Hear! Hear!" Jeremy cheered. "I told you," Jeremy said to Darien.

"Told him what?" Safire asked.

"I see it," Darien replied, ignoring the look he got from Safire.

"Let's get dessert," Angelina said, drawing Safire away.

After dinner was over, the boys went back to their game. Jeremy and Angelina headed out, and Darien stayed to help Safire clean up the kitchen and to talk to her. They didn't say much as they loaded dishes into the dishwasher, but after that, Safire made some tea for him, and they sat at the kitchen table to talk.

"I'm staying with Philly and Alex tonight, so if you want to talk, it has to be here."

"I want to talk," Darien said, not sure where to start.

"Okay," Safire said, "talk."

"First of all, I'm sorry I jumped to conclusions last weekend. But you've never told me how you feel, and you've never told me if we're exclusive, so I just didn't know. I'd still like to hear those things from you. But I was wrong to get jealous of your sister's fiancé. Why didn't you just tell me who he was?"

"Because it shouldn't matter who he was—is. You should know me better than that by now."

"How can I know you when you don't tell me anything? I didn't know we were shopping for your sister's wedding. I didn't know that your younger brother is all of seven years old. I didn't know that you come to take care of him sometimes. I didn't know that you were leading the children's reading groups at the Heritage Center. I don't know how you feel about me. Your family doesn't know you plan to go back to school. How can I know you better, Safire, when you won't let me in?"

"I invited you to come meet my family once," Safire said in her defense.

"You didn't even tell me that the dinner party was here," Darien retorted. "You don't really tell me anything. That leaves me to guess based on what you do say. I know you love our intimacy, but I don't know how you feel about me. Apparently, you called me a boy toy to your roommate—"

"I didn't say that, and she shouldn't have said it, either. I called you a hottie, but you are a hottie. If I called you a boy toy, it was a throwback to my former days, not something I meant about you."

"That's good to know because I don't want to be your boy toy," Darien said, taking her hand. "I want to be with you."

"Look, I'll admit that I have a little trouble opening up—"

"A little?"

"Okay, a lot. But you have to admit that you jumped to a bunch of conclusions, all of which painted me in a negative light. If you think I'm a Jezebel—"

"I never said that."

"No, you just asked if I was only sleeping with you for the sex," she whispered, balling up her fists.

Darien loosened one fist and took Safire's hand. "Tell me," he said. "Tell me how you feel."

She let out a sigh and then shrugged. "I'm still finding out."

"Then tell me that right now it's just us and that you feel *something* for me."

"I shouldn't have to—"

"Please, Safire."

"Okay, yes." She said it begrudgingly, but it put Darien's mind at ease and brought a smile to his face.

"Then will you promise to open up to me more? Please."

Safire rolled her eyes and her head. "Okay, fine," she said. "And you. What about you? You have to stop flinging accusations around."

"I will," Darien said. "So we have a truce?"

"I guess," Safire said. She still seemed hesitant. "But the next time you call me ho, no matter how you say it, I'm out of here. I don't allow that."

"I didn't mean to call you…anything. But I understand. I'm down. So we can start again, maybe a little slower this time, and you'll let me in, really talk to me?"

Safire shrugged but said, "Okay."

"I missed you," Darien said. "It was only five days, but I did."

After a moment, Safire acquiesced. "I missed you, too."

Darien smiled and kissed Safire's hand.

"And you don't have to stop working at the Heritage Center," Darien said. "Even if things didn't work out between us, I would never do anything to drive you away from your volunteer work there."

Safire sighed. "Okay. I can stay on until the end of next semester, maybe the summer. I don't think I can do it when I'm back in school. I'm not a Superman like you."

Darien smiled at that. She finally had the right paradigm. He leaned over and kissed her until she kissed him back.

It was a hard-won, tentative truce, but Darien accepted it. Safire had only reluctantly yielded ground, but her final decree had yet to be made, and she was ready to leave at the first misstep. She still had sore spots after calling it off. But then, he still had sore spots because she had called it off.

At least she felt something for him. Darien prayed that it was enough to let her open up to him so that they could have a real relationship and enough so that he could really learn to trust her—trust her without thinking. Because whatever it was between them, he wasn't letting go.

Chapter 13

Safire got out of the shower and pulled on a short ivory skirt with a floral brocade pattern. She had on an ivory peach-skin tank top, and over that, she wore the matching top to the skirt, a short bolero jacket. Her hair was down and her face was done, so she slipped on her two-and-a-half-inch gold sandals and grabbed her gold clutch.

It was Saturday, almost a week after they'd made up, and the first time that they would be spending together since the argument. Safire wasn't sure that she'd made the right choice by getting involved again after all that he had implied when he first saw her with Jeremy, but something about this man drew her in against her will, even after she'd determined to refocus. In the end, she couldn't resist how sweet he was when they'd talked at the old homestead, and now she couldn't help being a little excited about their date. Darien had someone covering his classes at the Heritage Center, so they had the day. She wasn't sure what he had planned for the afternoon, but he rang her buzzer on time, and she went down to meet him.

He met her at the front door wearing blue jeans that had words written all over them, a white T-shirt and a multi-colored vest with a harlequin pattern on it. He was ever the sexy artist and had a big smile on his face.

They hugged briefly, and then Darien stepped back to

look her in the eyes. He didn't say anything, but Safire could see that his mind was working, gauging something about her or perhaps wondering what he had gotten himself into. He bent his head down and pressed his forehead against hers.

"My difficult one," he whispered. "Don't forget that you said you'd open up."

His low voice sent a tingle through Safire's body, but she didn't move. "I haven't forgotten," she said when she found her voice. Then she stepped back, cocked her finger in the air and said, "And don't you forget—"

"I haven't forgotten," he said and chuckled, knowing where she was headed and cutting her off before she got heated. Then he tickled her ribs until she smiled.

He wrapped his arm lightly over her shoulder, and they headed into the parking lot.

When the passenger side of Darien's car opened, Safire was surprised. Out bounded a younger man—someone almost her age—wearing blue jeans and a light pullover in deep purple. He had short braids pilled over his head.

Darien smiled with pride as they neared the car.

"Safire, this is my baby brother, Lawrence. Lawrence, this is Safire."

The two smiled at each other and hugged spontaneously. Then Lawrence got in the backseat, leaving the front door open for her.

"My mom's car broke down two days ago," Darien explained. "We have a list of errands to run for her. Should we meet later?"

"I'm already in the car," Safire said. "What all do we have to do?"

"Ugh," Lawrence groaned. "Doctor's office for prescription, pharmacy to fill prescription, dry cleaner's for church clothes, pet store for special dog food, department store for present for our cousin's baby shower *next month,* grocery store for who knows what. And I bet she'll call us while we're out for something else. I think she just wanted us to run her errands. The car is probably working fine." He laughed.

"That about sums it up," Darien said and chuckled. "But her car *is* in the shop. I picked her up from the garage after they towed her. Are you sure you want to do this, Safire? It's not what I'd planned."

He took her hand, and a shiver ran up Safire's spine. She nodded.

"I also need some art supplies," Darien said. "You need anything, baby bro?"

"That," Lawrence said. "Looker—two o'clock."

They were at a red light. Safire looked toward two o'clock and saw a cute young man, maybe twenty-one, in tight jeans and a leather jacket.

Darien looked as well and cringed. "You have *got* to stop pointing out men to me, Lawrence. I am *not* interested."

"Who said I was talking to you?" Lawrence said. "I was talking to Safire."

"Good looking out," Safire said. "High five."

She held up her hand toward the rear seat and Lawrence high-fived her.

"Oh, Lord," Darien groaned.

Both Safire and Lawrence laughed.

Safire winked at Darien on the sly and reclaimed the hand that had been holding hers. Darien winked back at her and smiled, so he understood that she was only bonding with his little brother.

"Now he's got you into this," Darien said to her. Then he looked in the rearview mirror. "I don't want her ogling good-looking men, either," he said to Lawrence.

"Hey, a body's got eyes."

"Oh, slow down," Safire said.

"What?" Darien seemed concerned.

"Ten o'clock. Off the chain."

"Woohoo," Lawrence howled. "You called it. High five." After they high-fived, Lawrence said to his brother, "I like her."

"Okay, but let's not do this all day."

"Okay," Safire said, "only nines and tens."

Safire had regained Darien's hand, and when she said *tens,* she drew her finger along his palm. Darien got it and smiled.

"Deal," Lawrence responded.

"Oh, Lord," Darien groaned again.

"You better not let Mom hear you say that. She'll drag your butt to church for—"

"I know. I know."

Errands took up the morning and early afternoon. They decided to stop for brunch before hitting the grocery store and heading to Darien's house. Safire had a great time with Lawrence, who was talkative and very sweet, especially in the way he adored his older brother.

"So, what are you going to do with your psychology major," Safire asked Lawrence over brunch.

He got a little serious for the first time that day. "I'm not sure. I'm thinking about going on in psychology, but I really want to work with young people in the gay community. I'm not quite sure how yet, but I know I'll need more education than I have now. Psychology or social work—I have to figure out which. I'd also like to start or to work for a national magazine for queer youth. Are you going to help with the artwork, Darrie?"

"Yep."

"And I can do some editing or something," Safire said.

"I have to finish school first."

"How come you don't work at the Heritage Center?" Safire asked.

"I do in the summers. I run a workshop and reading group for queer youth in the summer program. It's great."

Safire saw what Darien had meant when he said his little brother was a sweetie. "And the braids?" she asked. "Following in this one's footsteps?" She motioned to Darien.

Lawrence grinned and smoothed back his unruly stalks. "Not quite yet, but in a little while, I'll be getting there."

After lunch, they went to the grocery store, and then they went to bring everything to Darien's mother. Safire held her breath. She hadn't expected to meet Darien's mother today. She smoothed down her top and pulled at the hem of her skirt.

Lawrence put an arm around her. "Don't worry. Mom is cool." Yes, he was a sweetie.

And she needn't have worried. Darien's mother was sitting on the couch in her nurse's uniform when they got in, and a little dog came yelping toward them. Darien's mother got up and hugged her sons, and then she hugged Safire, bringing tears to her eyes. Darien was looking at her, so she fought them back, but he had noticed.

Mrs. James chatted with her while the boys put things away. She talked about the odd hours she worked and how hard it was to raise two boys alone. She asked Safire where she'd met Darien and where she worked. Though the conversation was nothing special, it felt special to Safire. It meant something to her to be sitting and talking with an older woman.

She realized this when they parted. Mrs. James nodded at Safire and told her she was a pretty one and to be good to her son. Then Mrs. James hugged Safire again, bringing tears to her eyes once more. Darien hugged his younger brother, and Safire and Lawrence hugged again, and then the two went back down to the car.

Darien didn't ask her anything, but once they were in

the car, he took her hand and kissed her gently. Then he exhaled heavily and said, "Where to?"

Safire smiled. What she'd planned completed their family odyssey.

"I thought we could take Philly and Alex to a movie. Maybe Lawrence would like to come."

"Baby brother has about six loads of laundry to do tonight, so no. But I'd be happy to go. What are we seeing?"

"I don't know. I usually let them decide."

"That's fine with me."

"Let me call them."

The boys were up for a movie, and Jeremy was there, so he and Angelina could have a little time alone.

It turned out to be a good night. Safire didn't particularly care for the movie—a children's spy flick—but she got to cuddle with Darien in the theater. After the movie, they went for pizza, and Darien got little Philly to talk about the movie and what he wanted to be when he grew up and how he liked his teachers. He also got Alex to talk a little bit about designing video games.

"If you need help with the artistic side of things," Darien said, "let me know."

"So, you're an artist?" Alex asked.

"Yeah, and I teach classes for adults on Saturdays at the Heritage Center, if you're interested."

"Maybe. I need to learn to draw better so that I can do the games I really want to do."

"I'll send some information for you with Safire, and we can customize your lessons to what you'll actually want to draw. Let me know."

Safire couldn't figure out very much about her cousin, but one thing was sure—he only seemed to open up to men. She thought about opening up with Darien herself. Maybe she was a bit like her cousin.

It wasn't that she was generally quiet the way he was,

but she didn't give away important details and tended to handle things on her own. She gabbed to no end, and she helped her friends through their issues, but she didn't talk abut her own personal affairs in any great detail—well, nothing that really mattered. She didn't have a lot of issues in her life that she needed to talk about, actually. For example, she didn't have man problems because she hadn't really taken men seriously. They were for fun and play, and when that was over, it just wasn't meant to be. At least until now.

She had been this way a long time. When she lost her parents, she handled it by not advertising it. It was easier to be strong when no one around her expected her to be anything else. When they lost their mom, she could still go to her dad, but when they lost him, it was only them. And Angelina had had to take on Philly and Aunt Rose, as well as Safire herself. She didn't need a depressed teenager on her hands along with a two-year-old boy and their aged great-aunt. Safire had helped with them until she went off to college, determined to make it on her own. Yes, she had been quiet a long time.

Only now, she did have man problems. She had someone in her life who was threatening her view of men as play. She wondered why she hadn't taken men seriously before. When she was young, she didn't need to. Her parents were there to encourage her to stay focused on her goals, and after they were gone, it took all that she had to do just that and do it on her own. She liked to have fun, but she didn't need anything more, and more could be complicated. More, as she found, could land you where she'd just been—in a spiral of losses. She knew enough about that.

Come to think of it, more also meant opening up. It meant someone might see you cry over a simple question about jazz. It meant having to talk about all those things that she kept hidden, things that were still easier to cope with hidden. Yes, she was used to being quiet. Safire glanced at Darien. She would have to change that, or she might lose this man over her own silence. She took a breath. She would try.

Within a week, Safire's pledge came back to haunt her. It was Wednesday, and after Darien got through at school and at the Heritage Center, he came to pick her up. They were going out for a bit, and then they were coming back to her place, where she would finish cooking for them.

Darien rang her buzzer at quarter after six, explaining that he let his class out a few minutes early. Safire was ready. She had on an indigo cocktail dress that came midway down her thighs and that had two spaghetti straps. She had a sheer bolero cover-up to go over it, and she'd put her hair up. She kept on her black pumps from work and carried her black purse. She wasn't sure what they were doing— perhaps a café or happy hour. But then, this was Darien. She should have known better.

When she got downstairs, he was there in khaki slacks and a plaid beige-and-blue shirt with a khaki vest over it. He kissed her and walked her to his car.

"Where are we going?" Safire asked.

"There's a hint on the backseat," Darien said, smiling.

Safire turned around and found a picnic basket.

"Now, you know I cooked."

"It's just snacks. We're going to Oleta River State Park. I didn't rent us a pavilion, but I thought we could find a nice place near the beach to have some refreshments and play a game I brought."

"A game?"

"Don't worry. It's not as bad as Truth or Dare."

Despite Safire's heels, they found an empty picnic table off the water, and Darien spread their blanket out on top. He'd brought chilled wine and soda, cheese and crackers, grapes and glasses. Darien got all the snacks ready, and poured Safire some wine.

"So, here's the game." He took a large deck of cards out of the basket. "Each card has a question, but if you'd like, you can change it to anything you want. Each person gets, say, two passes. After that, you have to answer everything. And you have to tell the truth."

"Oh, no," Safire grumbled. Then she sat up. "Okay, I can do this."

Safire cut the deck.

"Usually, you use dice to see who gets to ask the first question, but I'll let you go first."

Safire pulled a card. "Okay, it says, 'If you had to lose one of your five senses, which would you rather lose, and why?'"

"Is that what you want to ask me? Remember, you can change it."

"I'll keep it."

"Okay, I guess I would rather lose my sense of smell. I guess that affects taste, but in general, I would still be able to see, taste—a bit, touch and hear. Now, for my question." Darien pulled a card. "This says, 'If you could have written any movie, which one would it have been, and why?' But that's not what I want to know right now."

"Uh-oh," Safire said, seeing the glint in Darien's eyes.

"I want to know how many men you've been with and how old you were when you first slept with someone."

"Okay. How many? Twenty maybe. Twenty-five. Always safe. And how old? I was seventeen the first time."

"The year your mother died."

Safire nodded, surprised that Darien remembered.

"Maybe those are related."

"Hey, don't psychoanalyze me. Leave that to Lawrence."

Darien rubbed her thigh. "I just want to understand. That's all."

"Okay. My turn. I'm getting the hang of this." She pulled a card. "It says, 'Which famous person would you like to be for a day, and why?' Forget that. I want to know if you've ever had a sexual experience with a man—anything, not just the full monty."

Darien nearly choked on his soda, and Safire laughed.

Darien cleared his throat. "Once, in middle school, with my best friend, but nothing really happened, at least nothing that worked for me. We were fully clothed the whole time. He turned out to be gay."

"I see," Safire said and then chuckled.

Darien pulled a card. "'What animal would you most like to be if you had to spend the rest of your life that way?' Now," he said, "what I want to know is why you didn't tell me anything about your family or about volunteering to teach the reading groups at the Heritage Center or…anything?"

Safire sighed. "I'd rather you ask about whether I've ever had a sexual experience with a woman."

"That's coming," Darien said, smiling. "But this is what I want to know now."

"I don't know. I guess my family seemed so personal."

"But we'd been…together."

"I know, but—I guess I'm not used to opening up with people I date. It doesn't usually last that long."

"I know what my next question is."

"About volunteering. I didn't want you to think I'd done that to pursue you or be with you?"

"You did that to find out more about teaching kids."

Safire was surprised once again by what Darien remembered about her. "Yes."

"And?"

"I still have to see, but I love it so far."

They asked each other more questions—why she hadn't told her family about going back to school, what he'd done with the engagement ring he bought for the woman he dated after college, why he had chosen to pursue a career in art. They stopped when Safire looked up and saw that the sun was setting.

"We have to go," she said. "I still have to finish dinner."

"But I haven't gotten to the most important questions," Darien complained.

"You don't have to ask everything tonight," she said, getting up. "We can play again. Or you can just ask. I'll be more open."

Darien looked disappointed, but he conceded. He helped Safire pack up and drove them back to her apartment.

Safire deposited Darien at the dining table while she finished dinner. The salad was ready, but the ingredients needed to go into the pasta, which had cooled. She had cut up the cheddar and pepper jack into little cubes and was mixing it into the pasta along with a medley of vegetables she had already sautéed. Then it occurred to her.

"Do you eat cheese?" Safire called out.

"Not very often," Darien answered.

Safire stopped. She couldn't really get the cheese out now. It wasn't the end of the world, but it felt as if she had just ruined dinner, and it felt as if she was the most brain-less person on earth. She knew it didn't make sense, but she stood over the wooden bowl and started to cry.

She didn't know that Darien had come in and that he was standing there watching her. What had come over her?

"Hey," Darien said. He took her shoulders, turned her toward him and pulled her against his chest. "It's okay. It's just cheese. I do eat cheese sometimes, and I can pick it out if I don't want it."

Safire cried for a moment and then stepped back from Darien.

"I'm sorry. I'm not really domestic."

"That's okay. I don't care about that. But tell me why? You can cook, right?"

Safire nodded.

"But you don't," he said. "Why?"

When the reason dawned on her, Safire's face crumpled, and Darien pulled her into his arms again.

"I used to do stuff like this with my mother," she said between her tears, "and she's gone."

Darien held Safire while she cried, but she didn't let herself cry for very long.

"It's all right," he said. "You can feel whatever you feel around me."

"I'm okay."

"Are you sure?"

He held her chin and looked into her eyes. Then he kissed her. She kissed him back, wanting the comfort of his arms, his loving. His mouth opened over hers, and his tongue slipped between her lips. She held him closer and closer, running her breasts over his chest and wanting him.

She moved her hand between them. He wanted her, too.

"Make love to me, Darien," she said.

In response, he lifted her and carried her into her bedroom.

His lips touched each part of her body that he undressed— her shoulder, her breasts, her stomach, her thighs. When she stepped out of her panties, he knelt before her and parted her petals with his tongue, and then his hot mouth sucked her inside. A sublime torment spread through Safire's center. She moaned and nearly lost her balance, but Darien's hands anchored her hips.

Everything was different with this man.

She thought he would stop soon so that they could move to the bed, but he didn't. He turned her body so that her back was against the nearest wall. Then his supple mouth clamped upon her rosebud once again, sending pangs of enchantment through her body. Safire hadn't realized that she'd moved her hands up to her breasts until Darien's hands joined hers, grating tenderly against the hard nipples and sending sensuous sparks throughout her body.

Her hips tilted involuntarily, bringing her wet flower more fully onto his searching mouth. Soon Safire's body was ravished with sensation. She cried out Darien's name and began to shake while the throes of exaltation ripped through her.

It was different than ever before.

The instant Darien rose, Safire's hands were upon his clothes, pulling them from his body so that she could kiss his hard chest and feel his warm skin against hers. She pulled him to the bed and straddled his legs, feeling the fever building up within her again. Darien murmured as she rode above him. They tensed together and fell over the verge together, clinging to each other.

They held one another while they quieted.

It was different—more loving, more love.

Safire put on her robe and went to make them a tray with dinner. Darien had pasta and salad, and Safire had hers with a slice of ham. When they were finished, they held one another again. Safire knew one of the questions Darien hadn't asked. He wanted to know how she felt about him. Right now, she felt so much that it scared her, because everything was different with this man.

Chapter 14

Darien had on casual clothes—orange jeans and an orange athletic crewneck pullover with a brown vest and his bronze-and-black sneakers. He had also told Safire to wear comfortable, casual clothes, and he couldn't wait to see what her idea of "casual" clothing was.

She met him at his apartment early that Sunday, and when he let her in, she sprung into his arms, laughing. Without knowing why, he started laughing, too.

"Don't you own a pair of sweatpants or jeans?" he asked.

"First off, we're not working out. No sweatpants and sneakers for a date. And second off, my jeans aren't practical. I can hardly bend in them."

She was wearing orange capris and an orange peasant top made of a sheer fabric with a solid orange shell underneath. She had on one-and-a-half-inch strappy sandals in brown, and her hair was in a loose ponytail. She was simply beautiful.

"We look like orange pumpkins," Safire said.

"It looks like we coordinated this."

"How many colored jeans do you have?"

"Oh, don't come for the colored jeans," Darien said. "They're my staple, like your skirt suits."

"We are as different as we can be."

Darien put his arms around Safire and kissed her. "That can be a good thing," he whispered in her ear.

Safire murmured and wrapped her arms around Darien's neck, grabbing a bunch of his braids in her fist. "I like it when you do that."

"Oh, yeah? We better get a move on before you get ideas."

"Are we really going to pick our own food? We should have brought Philly and Alex and Lawrence and... everybody."

"Are you sure you're going to be all right in those shoes?" Darien asked.

"Yes, these are comfortable."

"Then we're off."

They got in his car and got on the road. "It's a long ride," Darien said, "so I have some music. And—" he reached into his satchel "—I brought the cards."

Safire smiled. She seemed to be smiling at everything today.

"Okay," she said. "But let's start with the questions on the cards at first."

"That might be a good idea," Darien said. "I want to see your face when you answer my personal questions."

Safire reached over and swatted him playfully. Darien caught her hand and kissed it, but she kept his hand, linking it with hers. As her fingers curled with his, Darien felt a warmth move into the pit of his stomach and had the feeling that everything was right between them. Safire pulled her hand back only to shuffle the deck of cards, pop a CD into the player and turn the volume down. As Smokey Robinson began to play, she found his hand again.

She had the deck on her lap, and she used her free hand to pick up the top card.

"This is for you. It says, 'If you could star in any movie

that's already been made, which would you choose, and why?' I like that question."

"That, I don't know. I would have to think about it more, but right now, I'm going to say it's either *Malcolm X,* because that was one deep dude, and I would love to memorize some of his words, or *Boomerang,* because Eddie Murphy got to get next to Robin Givens and Halle Berry, and he chose the right one in the end. I know that's lame, but that's all I have."

Safire had started laughing when Darien said *Boomerang,* and she hadn't stopped.

"Okay," Darien said. "Simmer down, kids."

Darien withdrew his hand from Safire's and reached over to tickle her ribs. She roared and then quieted down. *"Boomerang,"* she said as he collected her hand again.

"Okay, what's my question for you?"

Safire pulled a card and read it. "'If you could change something you did in the past—just one thing—what would that be, and why?'" She pouted. "Ugh. Why did I get the stupid one? Let's sec. I don't know."

Safire became thoughtful, and Darien thought he knew what she was thinking.

"You can't bring your parents back because you didn't do anything to lose them."

"I know. I can't think of anything. Oh. I've got it. I wasn't always there for my sister and brother, especially when I was in school. I would go back and decide to go to school from home to help out more."

"If they needed you, wouldn't they have called?"

"My sister's not like that. She takes it all on."

"I've been told that runs in the Lewis family."

They played cards until they got to where they were going—connecting farms that let you pick your own produce.

"Over the summer," Darien said, "we'll definitely bring

the wee little one, Philly. He can get all the stuff that grows close to the ground, like blueberries and strawberries."

"What do they have now?"

"Lots of vegetables. Not so many fruits."

"This place is huge," Safire observed.

"Let me know if your feet get sore or tired," Darien said, "so we can stop."

"I can keep up. Don't worry."

They started on ladders with pears, clementines and lemons. In the end, they had walked and played for miles. They had gotten winter squash, sweet potatoes and kale, which were high on Darien's list. They had also gotten kiwi and mandarins; these were just along the way. The last stop was the herbs, and Darien had a ball, all the more because Safire was there and seemed to be enjoying herself.

Darien still felt guilty. He shouldered the heavier parcels and tugged Safire's hand. "Next time, you can pick what we do. We can even go clubbing. I know you like stuff like that more, and I know I like some oddball things."

Safire stopped in front of Darien and touched his face and kissed him.

"I like this just as much. It doesn't have to be one or the other."

"I'm in, I think. Does that mean we're going clubbing?"

"And swimming and—"

"We went swimming in Palm Beach."

"I know," Safire said, "but I love seeing you in skintight bathing trunks." She looked him up and down. "Hottie."

Darien felt as if he was blushing but hoped he wasn't.

"And you're mesmerizing," he said.

"Enough rest," Safire said. "Where to now?"

"Now for our last round of weighing and paying and loading the car. I hope you know you have to take half of this home."

"You're kidding. I don't even know how to cook kale. Maybe some of the fruit, but that's it."

"We *have* to come back for summer fruit," Darien said. "After this, I thought we could go to a late lunch before going home. I checked online for restaurants, and there's one that seems okay heading back toward the highway."

"Okay," Safire said. Then she took off ahead of him.

Darien thought she just wanted to play catch, since they'd been doing a little of that on the farm grounds. He realized in time that she meant to get ahead of him to the scales and pay for this round of produce. No way. He caught her by the waist and turned her around. She kept trying to get away, and he kept catching her by the waist until they were both laughing.

"Fine," she said. "But I can contribute."

"I know you can," he answered. "Save it for your college education."

"You help Lawrence out as well, don't you?" Safire asked.

"Yes, I do, but he also works part-time."

"You're a sweetie just like he is," she said and hugged him.

Something about Safire was different today. She was smiling and laughing, and she was as sensual as ever, but these things weren't unusual. Part of it was all of the play and affection between them—play that wasn't leading to the bedroom, affection that just seemed to be how they felt for one another. The chemistry was still there. Darien could feel it in the way Safire stirred his loins and kept him simmering. Yet it was more than this. She was revealing more about herself; she was asking more about him. There was a connection between them. She was trying to let him in.

Darien wrapped his arm around Safire as they headed back to the car, grateful beyond words for the difference in this day.

Their late lunch was at a roadside country restaurant with old-fashioned checkered tablecloths, heavy wooden chairs and overflowing plates. Darien had mashed potatoes and vegetables, and Safire had meat loaf with all the fixings.

"So who would you be in a movie?" Darien asked as they ate.

"Boomerang," Safire said and chuckled. "I don't know. Maybe the Diana Ross character in *Mahogany.* She was full of life."

"And a fashionista," Darien said.

"You hush. Well, let me ask you one. What would you change if you could change one thing?"

"I guess I would change being a player when I was younger. But that might not count because it's not just one thing. If it didn't count, I would change one of those relationships that burned me so badly and decide not to get involved in the first place."

"Which one?"

"I guess the second one did more damage." Darien turned to Safire. "Why haven't your relationships lasted very long?"

Safire shrugged. "I haven't found the right one, and I guess I haven't really been looking for that. I want to finish school. I like being independent."

Darien knew that there was more, but perhaps Safire didn't know this. Until it dawned on her, there was no way for her to articulate it to him.

"Could I be the one?" he asked. "Could we last?"

"Maybe." She looked up, thinking, and then looked at him and smiled. "Maybe."

Darien wanted to tell Safire that he had fallen for her. He wanted to ask her if it would scare her away if he said he loved her. And he wanted her to say no so that he could tell her.

Instead, he nodded his head, settling for maybe.

They played cards again on the way home. This time Safire pulled her legs up under her, and Darien sheltered her thighs under his palm. When she laughed at one of his answers, he tickled her ribs again, but he also touched her face and her lips.

The affection between them was lighting a fire in them. By the time they got back to Darien's apartment, Darien was as turned on as Safire seemed to be.

They washed and separated their fruit and vegetables, loading Safire's into a fabric bag, until she started touching him. Before they were finished, she said, "I dare you," flashing her Cheshire cat smile. Darien was starting to love that smile and couldn't help smiling back. Safire said, "I double dare you," and he took her in his arms, kissing her gently as he lifted her against his body.

Safire wrapped her arms around his neck and murmured against his lips, pressing back against Darien's body. Finally, Darien broke their kiss and lifted Safire off her feet, letting her wrap her legs around his hips. He carried her to his bedroom, laid her on the bed and covered her with his body. It was early evening, but Darien knew they would be eating a late dinner.

Darien put down the chisel and mallet he'd been working with and picked up a piece of sandpaper. He was adding some detailing to the Safire piece, and it was finally coming together. He didn't have long to work on it tonight, but he had added some relief to the base and was smoothing out part of the main figure so that he could begin doing some inlay work and wood burning. This piece was now taking all the time he could spare, but it was his most complicated work to date. It seemed to be turning out well.

After about two hours, he covered it and turned to his table. A piece was clamped to one end, and it wasn't turning out quite as he had hoped. He studied his drawing for a little bit and then picked up one of his chisels to work. His bedroom studio was filling with larger pieces, and he was glad. This meant that he should be ready for his exhibition.

After a while, he stopped, dusted off his clothes and went into the living room, where he had his schoolbooks and papers spread out on the coffee table. He had reading to do for classes tomorrow, and he had articles to read for his final paper for Critical Studies in the Visual Arts. In fact, he had work to do for all of his final papers and projects, as well as the preliminary draft of his prospectus. It wouldn't all get done tonight.

At about two o'clock in the morning, Darien was beat, so he went to shower off the grit before going to bed. It had been two days since he'd seen Safire, since they'd gone to pick fruit and vegetables, but her scent was still on his pillow. He loved smelling her and turned into his pillow to inhale her aroma. It was starting to fade, which made the gnawing in his chest grow. He missed her, and it had only been two days. He fell asleep thinking about her Cheshire cat smile and wanting to hold her again soon.

Chapter 15

Safire had spent the later part of the morning grooming. She had washed and curled her hair, exfoliated her face, shaved her legs, painted her fingernails and toenails—the works. She finished her face and checked her hair. She had pulled the front part back into a barrette and let the back part hang down in curls. She felt pampered and sexy, and she hoped that she looked that way, as well.

She was wearing a salmon-colored cocktail dress made of taffeta. It had one shoulder and hugged her curves. The bottom hem hit her upper thighs, and the skirt was gathered at the sides to create crescent pleats along the front and back. It had a matching cover-up made of sheer organza that was long and had a pleat in the back. She was stepping out.

After a brief search in her closet, Safire sat in the chair next to her bed to put on her shoes. They were off-white leather with a floral-cutout pattern and open toes, and they laced up the middle. They had three-inch heels, but the front had a raised base, so she would be okay. After she got her shoes on, she transferred her purse to a matching off-white clutch. When that was done, she opened the jewelry box on her dresser and found long white dangling earrings. Then she opened her top drawer and found a large white cuff bracelet. She was done.

It was Sunday, and it seemed that Sunday had become

a day to spend with Darien. This time she hadn't been able to see him during the week, but they were making up for it by starting early. They would be spending the day together, as they had last Sunday.

Things were going well, perhaps too well. Safire wasn't used to this.

While she was waiting for Darien, Safire munched on some pretzels, went through the mail, made a few calls and paid bills. Once she finished, she began looking over the materials for her book club sessions. She waved to Janelle, who was on her way out, and that's when the buzzer rang.

Safire opened the door and waited for Darien, who appeared from down the hall, looking sexy as all get-out in a cobalt-blue athletic-cut suit, that one braid at his temple loose. She stopped herself from skipping down the hall and leaping on him, but she couldn't suppress a smile. When he got to the door, she put her arms around his neck and leaned up for a kiss. He kissed her, lifted her up and turned her around. After letting her down, he stepped back and appraised her in her salmon cocktail dress.

"You look beautiful," he said and kissed her again.

She twirled around and laughed. "You look crazy sexy," she said. She placed herself in his arms and felt his shoulders beneath the jacket of his suit. "Good enough to eat."

His brow wrinkled. "I hope you're not hungry. We don't eat until later."

"No, not unless you're on the menu. I had a snack earlier."

"I had breakfast, but I'll be hungry later," he said, ignoring her innuendo. "Are you ready to go?"

Safire grabbed her cover-up and clutch, and they headed out the door.

They were going to a Sunday-matinee performance of jazz at the Adrienne Arsht Center for the Performing Arts on Biscayne Boulevard. The building was large and elegant, and Safire was glad that she was dressed for the occasion. They picked up their tickets at the box office and found their way to the Knight Concert Hall.

There was a whole series of jazz events at the Adrienne Arsht Center. They both enjoyed jazz, so the concert was an easy choice. It was Safire's pick.

At first, they held hands, bopping to the music. Then Darien slipped his arm around her shoulder, and they continued to move to the music, their heads almost touching and their upper bodies rocking in unison.

"Oh, I loved that," Safire said as they walked to the car.

"So did I," Darien said. His hand was on her back, and he looked at her. "I saw you get a little teary at one point. Was that one of your father's favorites?"

"Yeah, how did you guess?"

"You told me about your father and jazz the first day we met."

"I remember."

Safire shook her head. She hadn't realized that Darien would remember all that she'd said about her father playing jazz albums, but it mattered that he did. She wondered why she had told him that the first time they had gone out on the first day they had met. She had also told him about cooking with her mother. She told him things that she barely knew herself. Something about him made surprising things come spilling out of her—like tears. It was a bit unnerving.

Darien opened the car door for her, but before Safire got in, he gathered her against his chest and kissed her forehead and then her lips.

"Where to next?" he asked.

"Now to a dinner cruise on Biscayne Bay," she said and gave him the address of their departure harbor.

"This is great. You planned all this?"

"It didn't take much. I hope you like it."

"I do," Darien said.

They boarded the cruise, and dinner was served soon after the departure. It gave them a chance to talk.

"You know," Safire said, "we haven't been swimming here in Miami yet."

"That can be our project for next weekend," Darien said, "but you know it's November already."

"That's all right," she said. "The water will be in the low seventies. I can live with that."

"Actually, so can I," he said, and they chuckled.

They talked about the concert and then made up questions for each other like the ones on Darien's deck of cards. After they finished eating, Darien scooted next to her to put his arm around her, and they kept talking, but now they could also touch a little. The dining hall had thinned because people were going up on deck to participate in the tour. Neither of them wanted to move, so they stayed and watched the horizon changing outside the starboard windows.

Safire cuddled closer to Darien and rested her head on his shoulder and her hand on his chest. It was hard and warm, and Safire wished it was bare so that she could feel it better. His arm was around her, and his fingers played over her hair, lulling her.

"Did you have pets growing up?" he asked.

"No," she said, "but I wanted them. Dogs, little ones, like the kind you can walk around with in your purse."

Darien laughed.

"It's true," she said. "They have a huge cuteness factor."

"Do you want kids?"

"Maybe someday. No time soon. My sister's raising our little brother. He's seven and started to have seizures earlier this year. I babysit every now and then, but even that's enough to show me all the responsibility involved. Right now, I want to finish school and have a life. I'll have a life with kids, but it'll be a different life. It'll be about them. What about you?"

"I do," Darien answered. "I guess I need to finish school and try to become established as an artist and maybe a teacher. I love the Heritage Center, but I might want to teach at the college level one day. But I definitely want kids—two or three."

"I can see you being great with kids," Safire said, tracing circles along Darien's chest.

"I looked after my brother a lot growing up. We were being raised by a widowed, and then divorced, working mother, so I had no choice. I didn't mind, though. He's not that much younger than me, but it still gave me experience taking care of younger people. So does teaching."

"The kids are great."

Darien took her hand from his chest and kissed her fingers. It was a simple gesture, but it sent a thrill vibrating through Safire's body. He replaced her hand on his chest and continued their conversation as if nothing had happened.

"You're good with kids, as well," he said, "and you'll be great with your own."

They talked about kids and a bit about their families and about balancing work and school. Before they knew it, the port was coming into view and the tour was over. They disembarked and walked a bit. Then they turned back.

At the car, Darien asked, "Where to now?"

Safire took hold of his lapels and backed him up against the car before he could open her door. She pressed her body against his and kissed him. She kissed him until he slid his tongue into her waiting mouth and claimed it with his own. His body thickened against her, and it made her needy for more.

When the kiss broke, she put her lips next to his ears

and whispered, "I want you, Darien. Take me home so we can make love. Please."

She felt his body leap against her and knew that he wanted her also.

Safire moved her head to look into Darien's eyes. "Is that okay?"

He exhaled. "Okay," he said. "You're like a siren—my siren."

Darien drove them back to Safire's place as the sun was setting. Janelle was still out, so they had the place to themselves for a little while. Safire drew Darien into her room and slipped his jacket from his shoulders. She felt the twitching bulge at the front of his pants and ran her hand over it until he groaned. She couldn't wait.

Darien began moving his hands over her body, and the heat growing inside her burst into a flame of desire. Soon he had one hand on her breast, raising the soft nipple into a sensitive peak. Then his other hand climbed up beneath her dress and massaged her already throbbing core.

When she could take no more, Safire pushed Darien away. She pulled her cover-up over her head, moved the shoulder of her dress over her arm and turned around to pull the garment down her body, leaving her in a strapless bra, a thong and heels. Darien was watching her, stupefied. When she moved to him and began removing the clothes from his body, he came to life again and helped her.

Once he was naked, she found a condom in her drawer and offered it to him. As he sheathed himself, she made quick work of her remaining garments and her shoes, and they moved as one to her bed. She climbed in and pulled him down after her, already aching for the feel of him inside her. Darien positioned himself between her thighs, poised just at her entrance. The delicate pressure and the promise that it held made Safire wet and ready, until she was thrashing against his member, trying to pull him inside.

"Please, Darien, please."

"Yes," he said. "Anything."

With that, he moved inside her, filling her as her slick walls yielded to his presence. His thrusts filled her over and over, and her sex pulsed harder and harder. Darien's hand found her breast again, and his lips covered hers again, multiplying her sensations. The movement of his chest sent sparks into her breasts, and the pressure of his lips filled her heart with tenderness. He was ravishing her—body and soul.

Darien spun his hips in a circle, and Safire's back arched off the bed. Her hips tilted to meet his lunges, and she cried out, unable to stop herself from clawing his back, unable to stop herself from clamping onto his mouth, unable to stop herself from growing taut and thick and ready.

A heavy shudder moved through her womanhood, and waves of excitement fluttered through her sex as she tossed and clung, as she flooded and peaked, as she fell over the edge.

Darien must have been waiting for her because as the contractions rippled through her, he moaned and became stiff, convulsing above her until a sharp spasm shook his body, and he poured his passion out inside her.

Darien moved to her side, and Safire put her head on his shoulder, cuddling against him. Safire was blissful, but she was not to remain that way for long.

After they rested for a while, Safire was the first to move. She leaned up on her elbow and kissed Darien on the lips, rousing him.

"Can I get you something to drink? I'm thirsty."

Darien returned Safire's kiss—first her eyelid, then her cheek, then her lips. There was silence between them as they stared into each other's eyes. The love and sweetness she saw in Darien's gaze made Safire hold her breath. She let it out when his rugged face beamed into a smile.

"Anything you have would be fine. I'm a little thirsty, too."

Safire threw on a robe and stepped into her slippers with the one-inch heels before going out into the hall.

When she got back, she found that Darien had put on his underwear and was sitting on the bed waiting for her. He took the soda she offered and drank half the glass.

"I was thirstier than I thought. Thank you. I don't know if I can stay. If I do, I have to get up early in the morning."

"That's fine," Safire said, sitting down next to him. "I have to get up early, as well."

"I can get up with you," Darien said, "and leave while you're getting ready. I hate to run off, but I still have some reading to do for class, and I'm teaching tomorrow afternoon."

"I understand." Safire smiled at his concern. It wasn't as if he was sneaking out on her.

Darien put an arm around her. "When can I see you again? Next Sunday?"

"I don't know. Next Sunday I'm going with my sister to do wedding stuff, so that won't work."

"What about before then?" he asked, kissing her shoulder.

"No, I'm on with my girls on Wednesday. I'm babysitting my brother on Friday. I have my book clubs at the Heritage Center. Saturday I have errands. Aren't you swamped, too?" she asked, running her fingers through his braids.

"Yeah, I am," he conceded. "I have research to do, papers and a thesis-proposal draft due, final projects coming up, the fund-raiser at the Heritage Center, my classes there, the exhibit."

"Well, let's just play it by ear. We'll find a time, if not this week then next week."

"Safire," Darien said, shaking his head. "I don't like the

idea of playing it by ear all the time. I want us to be the real thing, not a whenever-it-so-happens thing."

Safire felt the conflict creeping up between them, but she didn't want to spend the night arguing. She smiled and leaned over to kiss Darien's neck.

"Let's not spoil tonight," she said. "Let's talk about it after the second round." She gave him her alluring smile.

"Let's not turn this into sex right now," he said. "This is about us."

Safire walked her fingers up Darien's thigh. "I'm talking about us."

"So am I. I want a regular thing with you and to know when I'll see you."

"We can talk about that later," Safire said, hoping to avoid the avalanche that was coming. "Let's just be together now."

But the avalanche came anyway. "Must it always be about sex?" Darien said.

That got Safire's dander up. "Just because I'd rather make love than argue doesn't mean it's always about sex, does it? And this is a real role reversal, now, isn't it? Don't you like sex?"

"I didn't say that, and I love making love to you. I just don't want that to be more important than what we mean to each other." Darien shook his head, apparently deciding not to follow the path that he had opened. "Forget it. I shouldn't have said that. I love being with you that way. But I also want a whole relationship. So let's sit down and figure out when we can see each other next. Then we can play."

Safire felt as if she was being backed into a corner, and she didn't like it. First, Darien had returned to the idea that this was casual—just about sex—for her. Now he insisted that they set dates in advance and set one right that minute. That wasn't being reasonable. Safire was past the dander stage now. She was starting to get riled.

"If there's not a good time," she said, "it doesn't have to be right away. Let's just see."

"So we're back to playing it by ear," Darien said, standing. "I don't want to play it by ear constantly. I want to see you, date you. I don't want to be a romp here and there or an occasional booty call whenever you have the time."

Now Safire stood. "Here you go again with that nonsense. We don't have to be with each other every minute to be in a relationship. Do we?"

"I want someone who would at least *like* to be with me every minute."

"Well, then you need to go to the pound and get yourself a puppy, because I'm a grown woman."

"You're not as grown as you think—"

"Oh, no, you're not going there."

"I just did." Darien stopped and held his hand up. "Back up one minute because I wasn't talking about being together every minute. I was talking about knowing the next time I can see you, even if that's in a little while. That's not unreasonable."

"And it's not unreasonable to say that we have other obligations right now and need to make plans another day."

"Underneath this little squabble," Darien said, "is the issue of commitment. Are we in a committed relationship, Safire?"

Safire folded her arms. "Stop trying to box me in. I said I want to see where it can go."

"You've been seeing for weeks now. When are you going to make up your mind?"

"I'll make up my mind when I make up my mind, not because you push me into it."

"Tell me you don't have feelings for me, Safire," Darien said quietly.

"I'll decide what I feel when I'm ready," Safire replied.

"This is where your age is showing," Darien said. "You

want to play but not be for real. Something as simple as setting a date in advance so we'll know when we can see each other again is too much of an obligation for you. Saying that we're in a committed relationship is too much. You don't see that we can be more than—"

Safire turned and squared off with Darien. "My age has nothing to do with this. Not wanting to be backed up against a wall is the issue. If we can't spend a few days not knowing when we'll see each other, then we can't see each other. And if I can't come to a decision in my own time, then you don't need to wait at all. In fact, you can just leave."

"I don't need to be told to leave twice," Darien said. "And I won't be put out a third time."

Darien snatched up his clothes and began pulling them on.

Safire left the bedroom. She opened the front door and waited. Darien marched down the hall and out of her apartment without looking her way. Safire banged the door closed behind him.

It was a horrible end to a glorious day. But damn it if she was going to be talked to that way. And damn it if she was going to start setting a schedule because he wanted it that way. And damn it if she was going to be cornered about the kind of relationship they had.

Bitter tears bit into the back of Safire's eyes, but she refused to let them fall. Damn it. Just damn it.

Chapter 16

Darien had one foot on his mother's coffee table and the other ankle crossed over his thigh with a book for his contemporary art class open on his lap. Lawrence came in from the laundry room just beyond the kitchen and plopped down on the other end of the couch, throwing one leg over the arm of the sofa. He lifted his other leg and tapped his big brother's sneaker with his own.

"Mom's going to get you if she finds your foot on the coffee table."

Darien knew this and knew better, but he was in a rather foul mood and hadn't cared. He also hated being corrected by his younger brother and knew he was setting a bad example. He shifted the book, took his foot down from the coffee table and resettled the book to resume his reading.

"Somebody's in a snippy mood," Lawrence said.

"Don't you have laundry that you're doing?" Darien asked.

"Yeah. But there's nothing for me to do while the machines are going. I'm not doing it by hand."

Darien sighed and went back to his reading. In a moment his mother called downstairs. "I'll be ready in a few minutes."

"Okay, Mom," Lawrence yelled back.

Darien was aware of his own silence.

"It's Safire, isn't it?" Lawrence said. "How are things going with her? I like her."

Lawrence noticed everything, always had. Darien left his book open but turned to his brother. He didn't want to talk about Safire, but maybe he needed to. He didn't know how much he could tell his little brother, but he needed to tell him something.

"I more than like her, but things aren't going well."

"What happened?"

"We had a fight. She seems to think *serious* is a bad word when it appears next to *relationship*."

"Ouch," Lawrence said.

"You're just about her age," Darien said. "Is a commitment a bad thing to your generation?"

Lawrence chuckled in a way that made Darien see him for the first time as grown.

"First," he said, "though it may not seem like it because you helped to raise me, we're actually in the same generation. Second, *commitment* isn't a bad word, but it's not as typical as it will be later on, when we're older. You've been atypical in that regard. I think that comes from your raising me, as well. And third, I hope you had enough sense not to bring up her age."

Darien looked down, shamefaced, and Lawrence cracked up.

"That aside," Darien said, "how long does it take someone to decide if they want to be in a real relationship?"

Lawrence pulled his leg from over the arm of the sofa and turned toward his big brother. "So where does it stand now?"

"She told me to get the hell out, so I'm giving her space."

"Is that what she wanted?" Lawrence asked.

Darien winced and then pursed his lips. "In a way. She wanted an undefined, see-you-when-I-see-you kind of thing."

"But she still wanted to see you?"

"Yeah," Darien admitted. "Until the fight."

"So you forced her hand. Decide now or else."

Darien hung his head, wondering if that was what he had done. "I just wanted to know when I would see her again." Darien thought about it more. "She's lost both of her parents. I think that has a lot to do with it."

Lawrence nodded. Darien was speaking his language now.

"That could easily lead to fear of loving someone else. They could also leave."

"Exactly." That's what Darien had been thinking. That's why there'd been no long-term relationships in her life.

"In the meantime," Lawrence said, "you need to decide if she's worth waiting for and being with—without pushing, without forcing her hand."

Darien heard the tone of caution in Lawrence's voice and nodded.

"I'm giving her space. That doesn't mean I've given up completely. I think she needs time to decide what she wants." Darien turned to his little brother again. "You know, you're going to be a great psychologist someday," he said. "I'm proud of you."

"That means a lot to me." Lawrence smiled, and his face lit up. He was grown, but he was still Darien's little brother. "Thank you."

"No." Darien said. He reached over and tweaked Lawrence's cheek. "Thank you."

Darien heard his mother on the stairs. Lawrence got up and hugged his brother before going to check his laundry.

"Don't let Mom drive you crazy," he said.

"I won't," Darien said and winked.

Darien's mom had changed from her good church clothes into a simpler dress and more comfortable shoes. Her car was not working again, so Darien was taking her on errands and then to see if she could get her car from the shop. He was still out of sorts, but talking with his brother had helped, and he thought he could make it through the early afternoon without being a total grouch. It didn't help that it was Sunday, his day to be with Safire. And it didn't help that he was overloaded with work and needed this time to get some done.

After being his mother's chauffeur for a couple of hours and then taking them to a late lunch, he drove her to the garage where her car was being fixed. It turned out, luckily, that the vehicle was ready. Darien helped his mother with the bill, and then he hugged her before they separated, heading off in different directions.

While his mother's errands could be irksome, her presence calmed Darien's spirit. Now he continued alone, and now there was nothing to stop him from thinking about Safire—her exuberance and feistiness and the tenderness beneath that, her sensual sorcery and the rawness of her past. He wanted to touch the bruised places inside her that she hid from herself and make them whole, if only she would let him in. Instead, she had kicked him out. But life didn't slow down for him to mope.

His errands today had to do with the fund-raiser at the Heritage Center, which was almost upon them. He had to get to the post office to mail invitations to the people on their mailing list, and he had to stop at several businesses to confirm their contributions for the silent auction. He had to get programs from the copy place, and he had to stop at the caterers to make some final arrangements. He wished that they were holding the event over the summer so that he actually had the time to do all of this, but that was not the case.

Darien ran along on automatic, his thoughts turning to Safire. He understood the pressure that she was under—family obligations, work, volunteering, friends, her sister's wedding. It would only get more hectic for her once she went back to school. He could see why she might have been hesitant to set another date to see him right away. With Safire, though, it wasn't just about things being hectic. It was about not wanting to confirm whatever it was that they had. But Darien's feelings were real. That was why he'd wanted confirmation. That was why he'd pushed.

Darien finished his errands and went home. He had more things to take care of for the fund-raiser, and he started with those. He had to email their ad to the local papers and get information to one of their corporate backers. He also needed to email some information about the Heritage Center to one of the emcees, and he needed to finish the slide show that they would be presenting during the dinner and save it on a jump drive.

He got on the computer and started checking off the tasks, but he was thinking about what his brother had said about Safire—that he needed to decide if she was worth waiting for, worth being with without pushing. He wondered if he'd pushed her to decide about their relationship too quickly. But he also wondered if he had completely changed her mind about playing the field. He hadn't made her want to commit, and if she didn't want to commit, then she might be at least open to other possibilities, if not actively pursuing them.

Darien turned off his computer and took a breath. He would give Safire space to make up her mind. That was the best thing to do, especially now that they'd basically called it off. He didn't like this new trajectory, but he would give her some time. It would also be time for him to cool down and get his head around the whole idea of not pushing.

Darien grabbed a snack and started in on some of his work for school. After this, he changed into his work clothes and went into his studio. He had to get to the Heritage Center early tomorrow to set up slides and supplies for his class and to get some more work done for the fund-raiser. That meant he would be home late tomorrow, so he had to make the most of tonight. He had various projects clamped around his worktable and several sitting in the center.

The first thing he saw when he walked in, however, was Safire. Her influence was written all over his most recent pieces. It was in the sensuality of the lines, the uninhibited nature of the designs and the freedom of movement.

It troubled him—the way she'd insinuated herself into his art. It meant that Safire was on his mind whether Darien wanted her there or not. She was in his thoughts when he wasn't controlling them. She was in his head even when he didn't know it. He meant to give her space, but he didn't intend to pine over her the whole time he was doing that. Yet here she was—in his art.

Darien shook his head and started to work on one of the pieces for his figure-sculpture class. On a pedestal in the center was an auction block with three nude figures— Africans being sold who had been stripped of everything but their headpieces and who were trying to cover their nakedness. The base of the pedestal was an African family tree, and around the base on a downward slope were figures of their descendants, those from slavery and afterward. His goal was to convey the movement of each figure and to tell the story of the family. The central figures were done. Now he was working on the descendants. And right under his eyes, Safire's face appeared on one of the figures.

Darien put down his chisel and shook his head. If he was going to give her time, he would need to get her out of his mind. But he couldn't. If nothing else, there was still the piece of art he'd started—the Safire piece—which he hadn't finished. Maybe if he could finish it, if he could finally capture Safire, then he might be able to stop being surprised by thoughts of her and just give her the space that she needed.

Darien went to the piece in the corner and uncovered it. It was time to finish it. But that wasn't going to be easy. As he'd worked on it, it had kept getting more complicated. It was now ready for him to add some metal and ceramic parts. He could do the metalwork tonight and start the ceramic pieces in the morning if he got up early.

Darien took out his soldering iron and some metals, replaced his goggles and began working with a vengeance. One way or another, regardless of whatever else he had to do, he was going to get this sculpture done and take a break from Safire Lewis.

Chapter 17

"Here," Safire said, taking the handheld game from Philly. "Let Alex play for a little while." They had just taken off for Charlotte on their way to Houston, and since they'd had to get up early for the flight, Philly was a little tired. "Come put your head down," she said to him and pulled his head against her arm.

A couple hours of sleep on the flight to Charlotte would do him good. They didn't want to stress him for fear that he would have another seizure.

"Are you sure?" Alex said, taking the game from her.

"Go ahead. Philly needs a little more sleep."

"Cool," Alex said.

Angelina and Jeremy were across the aisle from them. Jeremy had his arm over Angelina's shoulder, and she was cuddled against him with her eyes closed. Safire could see that their other hands were linked and that Jeremy's fingers were slowing massaging Angelina's. They were such a sweet couple, and it was so cute the way her sister got embarrassed by their affection. Safire sighed, a little jealous of that affection, especially since she herself no longer had a possibility on the horizon.

For the briefest moment she imagined what it would have been like if Darien was there, his fingers intertwined with hers. She ached for his touch, his smile. Maybe she should have set a date; it was sweet of him to want to know when he would see her. But she still felt she had been boxed in, that she was being forced to say things she wasn't ready to say as yet. There were so many maybes. All she knew at that moment was that she wanted his arm around her, his presence in her world.

Safire put the thought from her mind. She made sure her brother was sleeping and took out the book for her older reading group. She had to find a good selection of *The Women of Brewster Place,* and the novel kept her occupied until they got to Houston.

When they arrived, Jeremy's younger brother picked them up from the airport.

"Hey, biggie," he said, hugging his older brother.

Once the guys were finished, they stepped apart, and Jeremy introduced everyone.

"Eddy, this is my fiancée, Angelina." The two hugged. "This is her sister, Safire."

Safire put on her game face; she didn't want the others to know how heavy her heart felt. "Hey," she said, trying to sound upbeat. "I've heard we have a lot in common. And you're a cutie, too, just like your big brother."

"If we have a lot in common," Eddy said, "we have to hit the clubs. It's Thanksgiving weekend. Everyone and their mother will be out."

"I'm game, and I brought my going-out shoes," Safire said, getting hold of her large suitcase and dragging it down from the baggage carousel before Eddy took it for her. She wasn't up for going out, but there was no use sulking at home. Plus, she didn't want Angelina to think anything was wrong.

"Don't struggle," she said to Eddy. "It has wheels."

"Don't be a bad influence," Jeremy said to his little brother.

"Hey, we're just going out. Maybe you'll come with us now that your dance partner is here."

"Maybe," Jeremy said, thinking about it. "This little one is Phillip, Angelina and Safire's brother." Philly got shy and just stood there until Eddy smiled and bent down to shake his hand.

"You got a nice grip there," he said to Philly.

"Hi," Philly said.

"And this is Alex, their cousin," Jeremy said.

The boys shook hands. "Are you twenty-one yet?" Eddy asked.

"Almost."

"Oh, you might have to sit this one out."

"That's fine," Alex said.

"This," Jeremy said, "is my scandalous baby brother, Edward. Eddy for short."

Safire acted mechanically, putting on her old, buoyant demeanor. She put her hands on her hips and eyed Eddy. "You don't seem too scandalous."

"The oldsters don't know what scandalous is."

"Word," Safire said. "That's just what I was thinking."

"And just so you know," Eddy said, "we're going to have to do this all over when we get home."

The grown-ups chuckled, except for Safire, who managed a tense smile. It hurt even to do that, and she hoped no one noticed anything out of place.

"Who's at the house?" Jeremy asked his little brother.

"Only the parents and grandparents—so far."

"Well, let's go."

When they got to the house, it was still only the four elders, thankfully. Jeremy started by introducing Angelina, his fiancée, and Safire, her sister. But that was as far as he got. His mother's hands went up, and she took hold of Angelina, and his father gathered Safire in his arms. Safire was frozen in a warm and genuine fatherly embrace.

Before Safire could understand why, tears were pouring out of her eyes, and when she looked at Angelina, tears were running down her sister's face, as well. After they were released, Safire and Angelina went immediately to each other, still crying. The second they broke apart, the opposite parents got hold of them, and it started all over again with Safire encircled in the hold of Jeremy's mother and Angelina engulfed by the arms of Jeremy's father. And the two girls were crying all over again.

"Oh," Mrs. Bell said, dabbing at her cheeks. "You girls got me going."

The four released each other, but tears were still flowing down Safire's face. She looked at her big sister, who was just beginning to get hold of herself. Jeremy had stepped in as his father let her go, and now Jeremy held her.

"It's been a while since we've had parents," Angelina explained.

"Sorry to make a spectacle," Safire added.

Angelina stepped out of Jeremy's arms and came to her. They wrapped their arms around each other, and Safire continued to cry. There was so much inside her fighting to come out—what it meant to have the embrace of a parent, what it meant to have lost a lover. All of her feelings were bustling with each other for release. Old wounds that had been buried jostled against the new amputation that she had been trying to hide. The circle of loss rose around her, sheltered by the love of new parents and her gratitude for their welcoming arms. For a moment, she could miss her mom and miss her dad and miss her great-aunt and miss Darien. For a moment, she was able to let herself feel those heartbreaks.

Safire finally shook her head and pulled herself together so that Angelina would stop fussing over her.

When it was done, Philly came over to Angelina and

hugged her legs. It was clear that he wanted to make sure she was all right. Alex and Eddy hung back, observing it all.

"We'll do the rest of the introductions over lunch," Jeremy said. "We're taking all of you out."

Safire and Angelina greeted Jeremy's grandparents and went to the couch to give them brief hugs.

"Come, girls," Mrs. Bell said. "Let me get you something to drink before we head out."

"And you boys have to see the grill now that she's done," Mr. Bell said. Jeremy and Eddy smirked but obeyed their father. Jeremy lifted Philly onto his hip and followed his father outside.

In the kitchen, Mrs. Bell poured Safire and Angelina lemonade and touched their faces. "My, don't you both look like sisters. I never had a girl. Now I have two. Before you go back, I have a couple of things for you," she said to Angelina. "There's something old and something borrowed. The three of us can go shop for something new and something blue."

Safire recalled her hope to have Darien as her date to the wedding. That wouldn't happen now. She felt a sharp pang, but she nodded and made her face neutral.

When they got back to the living room, they helped Jeremy's grandparents into the car and called the boys.

"Angie," Philly said excitedly, "can we have a puppy?"

"The neighbor's dog's just had a litter," Jeremy explained. "They're in the adjoining yard out back."

"We'll see," Angelina said. She patted Philly's head and used it to guide him toward the door. She also took hold of Alex's hand and petted it for a moment. "You okay, sweetie?" she asked him.

"Yeah. I'm fine."

"Then let's go," Jeremy said, wrapping his arm around Angelina.

Safire felt another twinge, another gaping whole where

Darien would have been. She brushed it off and smiled, and they headed out.

They took two cars and went to a late lunch. On the way back, Mr. Bell took the grandparents home, and Eddy drove the rest of them back to his parents' place.

Before long, the buzzer started ringing, and soon Safire found out why Jeremy had asked how many people were at the house, which started filling up with remarkable speed. Neighbors, church members, coworkers and relatives started popping in to see Jeremy and his new fiancée. Mr. Bell fired up the grill. Jeremy and Eddy donned their sweaters to carry the trays of meat back and forth while Safire and Angelina helped Mrs. Bell in the kitchen and got drinks.

When Alistair and Reggie got there, Jeremy and Angelina took a break to be with Jeremy's friends, and Alex took their son, Tyler, and Philly up to one of the bedrooms so he could watch them. Jeremy's friend Michelle also came over. She and Alistair were home for Thanksgiving. They both knew before Jeremy did that his mother was planning a gathering.

At about ten o'clock, Eddy pulled Safire over to the side.

"How about we get out of here? You feel like a club?"

Safire didn't feel like going out, but she made her face a mask and managed to chuckle, seeing the resemblance between them. "Okay, but I can't stay long. I have to help clean up."

"Unless you meet a handsome stranger." He winked at her.

"I can't ditch the in-laws," Safire said. "I just met them. What kind of impression would that make?"

"Don't worry. I got you covered. It was late, so we decided you would come over by me. It's airtight."

Safire made her lips into a smile. She liked the plan; in

fact, it had her signature written all over it. But she also knew she wasn't up to meeting anyone tonight.

"Let's just go to the club, and then you get me home early so I can help Mother Bell. We can be scandalous another time."

Eddy shrugged. "Whatever you say. But if you change your mind, remember the plan." He turned toward the kitchen. "I'll go let the folks know we're checking out."

Jeremy came over and gave his little brother a warning stare. Eddy and Safire plastered innocent looks on their faces.

"Okay," Jeremy said, "but you look out for her out there, and don't let her run off with any strangers in a strange town."

"I don't know if I'm the one you have to worry about," Safire said. "I'll keep an eye on *him*."

"That won't work," Angelina said. "That's the pot," she said, pointing to Eddy, "and that's the kettle," she said, pointing to her sister. "We're not apt to see either one before noon tomorrow."

"Y'all get back in time for Thanksgiving lunch," Mrs. Bell said, coming from the kitchen. "You're a gentleman," she said to her younger son. "You watch out for the young lady like I taught you right."

"Of course I will, Mom," Eddy said with an angelic smile. As soon as his mother went back to the kitchen, it twisted into a smirk.

"Let's go," he said. "You'd think we were twelve the way they go on."

"Should I change?" Safire asked. She was still wearing the short, navy skirt suit and light turtleneck she had travelled in.

"It get's colder here at night, but I have a couple scarves in the car. You look fetching. Hey, you might have already met that handsome stranger."

Safire contorted her face and cringed. "You're almost my brother."

"Almost doesn't count." Eddy opened his car door for her.

"Yes, it does," Safire said. Eddy was a looker, like Jeremy, just younger and a little shorter. He had the same suave look, only in a more boyish face. If it wasn't for Darien, she might have considered his invitation, but now she couldn't think of it. "Let's go."

They went to a club called the Mixing Pot, and Eddy got drinks for them. It was nice to be in a club again for a change. The Mixing Pot had a long bar, raised tables around the edges of the room, soft sofas in front of lit fireplaces, television monitors showing dance videos, loud music, disco lighting and large dance floors. Safire didn't feel like it, but she mustered her grit and put on her party mode.

After a few dances with Eddy, she caught him looking at a woman and interceded for him. Of course, the woman said yes to a dance, cutie that Eddy was in his red turtleneck and jeans. That left Safire to hold down the table where they had their drinks. Now she knew why she wasn't up for this. It was nice to dance, and the music was good, but she wasn't looking for a dance partner. She'd just had a dance partner at home—Darien.

Safire found herself staring at her drink, not even moving to the music. This wasn't like her, but she didn't know what to do other than try to put Darien out of her mind. He wanted a declaration, a commitment and a schedule. She wanted him, wanted him like no one ever before, but she wasn't going to be commandeered or corralled, and she sure as hell didn't need someone setting a schedule for her, not with what she had on her plate already. These facts didn't help her right now, though. She thought of slow dancing with Darien at the Grotto, and she didn't want anyone else.

A young man wandered over to her. He smiled and nodded in the direction of the dance floor. Safire wasn't in the mood. She pointed to her drink and shook her head. This happened three more times during one song. Finally, Safire gathered up her drink and Eddy's drink and found a seat on one of the sofas in front of a fireplace. She crossed her legs, sipped her drink and looked at the dancers.

From where she sat, Safire could hear the slow music coming from another room. If Darien was there, that's where they would be. Safire shook her head. This brooding wouldn't do. It wasn't her. It never had been. She coped by using determination, by remaining vital. When she finished her drink, she found a partner and danced the next set just to do something. When that was over, she was ready to go.

She found Eddy on the dance floor with the woman she'd pointed in his direction and told him she was going to take a cab home.

"No, I'll take you," he said above the music. "Do you mind if my new friend rides with us?"

Safire shook her head. He worked even faster than she did before she'd met Darien. And there was that name again. At the car, Eddy offered to take them for dessert at an all-night diner. It was still early, and Safire didn't want to ruin Eddy's fun, so she agreed. At the diner, it was clear that Eddy's new friend would be going home with him. Safire asked them to drop her off on their way, which they did. Eddy even walked her to the door.

It occurred to Safire that this was what Darien thought of her, and not too long ago, he wouldn't have been far from wrong. She liked to go out and to meet new people, and she didn't really get serious. She could see why Jeremy had said that she and Eddy had a lot in common. Only they didn't have quite so much in common right now.

"You be careful," Safire said as he left her at the door.

"I always am," Eddy smiled and winked.

"And be up front," she warned.

"I'm always that, too." He smiled and turned and left.

Safire could see herself in Eddy. And she wasn't sure she liked the image. Eddy had a couple of years on her, but perhaps she was starting to outgrow the casual club scene. Or perhaps it was just Darien.

It was just after one o'clock when she got in, but the family was up cleaning. Safire took off her blazer and helped load the glasses into the dishwasher, while Angelina and Jeremy did the pots in the sink. Jeremy's mother came in with a load of plates.

"You go to bed, Mom," Jeremy said. "We've got this."

"If you're sure, honey."

Mrs. Bell hugged her son, and then she hugged Angelina and Safire, and Mr. Bell stepped in to say his goodnights, as well. The trio finished up in the kitchen, and then Safire and Angelina went to Eddy's old room, where their things were.

Jeremy detained Angelina at the door. "You know you can come sleep with me in my room," he said, kissing her.

Angelina swatted him. "Not in your parents' house. We're not married yet."

"They won't care, love."

"Maybe after we're married."

Jeremy chuckled, kissed Angelina on the head, waved to Safire and padded down the hall to check on Alex and Philly in the spare bedroom.

"You are practically married," Safire said.

"Do you mind the company?" Angelina asked.

"No, of course not. I'm just saying."

Angelina started changing into a long, floral nightgown. "You weren't out long," she said.

Safire slipped on some sweats. "I wasn't in the mood."

"If I didn't know better," Angelina said, "I'd think it was that sweet young man we met. What is his name?"

"Darien," Safire said, knowing it was him and wondering if Angelina had seen through her facade. "I guess it's him. We had a fight, and I told him to leave—again."

Safire was tearing up a little thinking about it. This wasn't like her, but neither was how much she missed this man. Angelina noticed and put an arm around her little sister's shoulders. "It'll be okay. If he's anything like Jeremy, he'll be back."

"I think I wrecked it this time for good," Safire admitted.

"Then perhaps you should make the call and fix things."

Safire had always kept her cool about men and was surprised by all the reactions this relationship was getting out of her. But there was something about being in a home, a home with parents in it. It made all of her vulnerabilities come out; it gave her a safe place to release them. And she had to admit that she'd been feeling more vulnerable since her latest breakup with Darien. There was pain and longing in her heart.

"He pressed me for a date that we would meet again, and then he pressed me to define our relationship."

"How long have you been seeing him, sweetie?"

"A few months," Safire answered.

"Wow," Angelina said, pulling back the covers for them. "That doesn't seem like an egregious request."

"Maybe. But he can make me so angry." Safire sighed. "Just when things were going so well."

"Maybe too well," Angelina replied, getting in bed. "Did you sabotage it?"

"I don't know. Maybe."

"You never let it get serious, Safire. Maybe this time it is—or you want it to be."

Safire got into bed. She didn't like what her sister was saying, but she couldn't argue against it, not at the moment. She looked at her sister.

"Thanks, Angelina."

"You're my sister, sweet pea."

Safire turned off the light. "You're my sister, too. Jeremy's parents are really nice."

"I know," Angelina said. "We sure did let out the waterworks this afternoon. I guess it's been a while since we've had parents, both of us."

"I know," Safire said. "It's nice to be here with them."

Angelina turned over. "Let's get some sleep."

Safire pressed her palm to the void in her chest and let her sister get some rest while she dwelled on the man who had moved her—body and soul. When she got up late the next day, Angelina was already dressed and gone. Safire showered and emerged in time for Eddy's arrival with his grandparents. Both got teased for being late risers.

The rest of Safire's time in Houston was as hectic as the first day. Thursday it included Thanksgiving lunch with Jeremy's family, helping Mrs. Bell with dinner, and dinner itself, followed by football and cleanup. The next day, it included shopping with Angelina and Mrs. Bell for something new and something blue and going out that night with Angelina, Jeremy and Jeremy's friends. Safire tried to enjoy it all but couldn't.

Eddy offered to take her clubbing two more times, but she declined. Yet there was still more than enough to do. Saturday, Eddy took her on a tour of the city, and they met the family for a late lunch before taking the kids to a movie. They got home in time for more Thanksgiving leftovers and to let the travelers prepare for their journey home.

When Safire got back to Miami on Sunday, she was more tired than when she'd left, but it was so nice to spend time with a whole family, one with parents. It filled a space in her that was empty. Another slot was still blank.

Two days after she got back home, Safire ran into Darien. She'd had inquiries about one of her school applications. They needed more information from her to consider her request for funding. They also had a reading that they suggested she attend. They couldn't tell her yet if she'd gotten accepted, but all of this was a good sign. After the reading, she decided to stop in the bookstore and look at the books for classes she hoped to be taking the next fall. It couldn't hurt to get ahead.

She knew that Darien went to Florida International University, but it was huge, with over fifty thousand students. There was no need to worry that she would see him there. She wasn't going anywhere near the Art Department.

It turned out that the author of a new book on art was having a reading and signing at the bookstore, and there was Darien, along with a cadre of his artsy friends. He hadn't seen her amid the bookshelves, and she had found a book that she wanted, so she was ready to slip out before she was spotted. She couldn't face him—not yet. And if it hadn't been for one of the women in Darien's group, she would have gone.

The woman was blonde, with her hair tied up in an African wrap and a mud-cloth cape on. That by itself was enough to spike Safire's temper. But when the woman put her arm around Darien right where they stood at the book signing, Safire got fully piqued. She had no right, she knew, but she couldn't stop herself from going to stand up in Darien's face, pointing out, just with her presence, what a hypocrite he was.

Safire stood directly in front of Darien. "Long time no see," she said with her hand on her hip.

Darien straightened, looking surprised to see her and perhaps by her tone. His smile was momentary and then vanished. "Yes, it's been a little while." He turned to the woman at his side, "Would you excuse us for a moment?" Then he took Safire's elbow and walked her away from his group and the signing, leading her toward the cash registers.

"A bit testy today, are we?" he said.

"Just noticing how long it took you to find someone else," Safire said.

"She's not someone else, and we're not involved," he said calmly. Then he added with a hint of warning, "And I'm not going to fight with you here like we're six-year-olds. If you calm down, you can stay. Otherwise, you should leave."

"Don't you usher me out the door. You don't own this place."

"No, I don't," Darien said. "And I can't stop you from being here, but I don't want to argue with you. Calm down, and come meet the author. Meet some of my classmates. But if you're in a huff, forget it."

Darien's calm and his apparent embarrassment over her just infuriated Safire more. "I'll be in a huff anywhere I choose."

She was at the register now, so she paid for her book.

When she turned around, Darien was gone. She had a mind to go look for him and read him the riot act, but she thought better of it. This was not how she had imagined a meeting between them would go, not when she'd been pining over him. Safire clutched her book under her arm and stomped out the door.

Chapter 18

Darien left his professor's office feeling relieved—at least about school. He was on the right track with his prospectus and final exhibit plan and would be able to finish up the prospectus next semester. He had submitted his projects for his figure-sculpture class and his final papers for his Caribbean art class and his contemporary art class. Now he only had to finish up his final paper for Critical Studies in the Visual Arts, and his semester would be over, leaving him time to finalize his exhibit and a couple of weeks to get ready for the Christmas holidays, which he hadn't yet considered.

He was on his way to the library to do more research for his last paper when he thought about Safire. He hadn't expected to run into her at the bookstore, and she obviously hadn't expected to see him, especially not while Alicia, one of his classmates, was hanging on his shoulder. In a way, it was a dose of her own medicine. She was the one who didn't want to define their relationship. In any case, he didn't want to fight with her when he was supposed to be giving her space. He'd left her at the register without even saying goodbye; that would only have continued their dispute.

He did expect to see her tonight, which was Friday and the night of the fund-raiser at the Heritage Center. It was a gala dinner and fund-raising event, and she would be there either as one of the volunteers or with the table purchased by the Law Offices of Benson and Hines.

Darien finished at the library, taught his class at the Heritage Center and went home to change for the evening event. He decided on a dark purple suit and a kente cloth tie with a purple theme. Since he would be presenting a few of the awards and talking about some of the work of the Heritage Center, he figured he should dress. Safire would doubtless be decked out; it was the perfect occasion for the fancy end of her wardrobe.

Darien got to the gala early. He needed to get the programs, awards, donation envelopes, slide show and his talking notes from his office, and he needed to make sure that the caterers were setting up, that the silent-auction items were being put out and that the volunteers were decorating. The event was being held in the lecture hall at the Heritage Center, but by the time he walked in, you couldn't tell that it was a lecture hall because it was so done up—covered tables, floral arrangements, the works.

Mr. Johnson came in not long after he did, and together with the volunteers, they got programs and donation envelopes on the tables and started the slide show running in time for the first handful of their two hundred guests. This included their two emcees for the night—a local actor and a local radio host, both of whom could boast of time spent at the Heritage Center as children.

Since it was late, the program started with the repast, the slide show and bidding for the silent auction. Darien noticed Safire sitting at the table for Benson and Hines. She was wearing a short embroidered cocktail dress made of chartreuse fabric. It had no shoulders or straps and fit her like a coat of paint on a car. Over that she had a sheer chartreuse bolero cover-up with feathers over one shoulder and at the bottom hem. She wore three-inch heels, and her hair and face were done to perfection. She was breathtaking. Darien stared at her and sighed, but when she glanced his way, her face changed to thinly veiled disgust, and she looked away.

The emcees started the program during dessert. After acknowledgments, Darien was called up to talk about some of their activities. Next, students were called up to give testimonials about some of the classes, and then a call was made for the filling of the donation envelopes. Mr. Johnson reported on their fiscal matters and thanked the corporate backers and the volunteer entrepreneurs and the attorneys. Then Darien gave the awards for outstanding work to some of the students and volunteers.

Safire was one of the volunteers being awarded that night. She had accepted an award for Benson and Hines earlier. This one was for her.

"The next award," said Darien, "is a special one. It goes to an outstanding volunteer teacher as voted by participating students. This year that award goes to Ms. Safire Lewis for her work reigniting the Book Club Program for children aged eight to twelve and thirteen to sixteen. *Both* of Ms. Lewis's classes voted her outstanding volunteer teacher."

Safire approached the podium like a model, wearing a bright smile. But as she neared Darien, her smile turned cold, plastic. She accepted the engraved glass plaque with a curt thank-you and turned from him without another word.

After Darien had given all of the awards, the emcees called for a twenty-minute break so that final bids could be made on the silent-auction items. They spent the time talking about the items—which ranged from student artwork to airline tickets. It was a silent auction, so people were encouraged to go take a look and write down their bids.

Darien's path wandered across Safire's path as they were looking at the auction pieces.

"Hello, Safire," Darien said.

"Mr. James," she returned.

"Congratulations on your award. You were student picked, which is something."

"Thank you," she said and turned to walk away.

Darien was supposed to be giving her space, but he couldn't help wanting to pull her back and take her into his arms.

"So we've gone from arguing to the cold shoulder?"

"If that's what you call it."

Maybe she still needed time, but Darien was starting to wonder how much. He would have loved to have been together with her at this event, to have her as his date. Nothing in her expression signaled that she felt the same way, except, perhaps, her continued rage over seeing him with Alicia's arm around him.

"My brother's here," Darien said, "and so is my mother. They're at the table next to the head table. Maybe you'll go say hi."

Safire looked past him noncommittally and continued to peruse the auction. She wrote her name and bid down next to a child's toy, probably for her brother, Philly, and continued around the room. As she neared the front, however, Darien saw her leave the auction tables and hug his brother and his mother.

Darien had been called over to talk to some of the businesspeople, so he couldn't go to them, but he was glad that Safire went to greet his family. And he was wondering again how much time she needed.

When the program was almost over, the emcees invited Mr. Johnson up to make one final call for the filling of donation envelopes.

"Anything you can give helps the programs that you've heard about at the Heritage Center. Thank you."

Then they announced the winners of the silent auction and told how much money it had raised. They also announced how much was made that evening, which was almost seventy-five thousand dollars.

"That includes tickets, the auction, donation envelopes, mail-in donations and corporate sponsors. If you'd like to make it an even seventy-five, just come up to the podium."

The last thing was a live song, and a local ensemble went up to sing "Lift Every Voice and Sing." Then the emcees said good-night, and people started filing out.

Darien didn't see Safire again after the gala. She slipped out while he was greeting parents and people from the local community, probably to give him his comeuppance for leaving her in the bookstore. He stayed behind to collect extra programs and begin cleaning up. How much time did she need?

Two days later, Darien was still wondering about this question. It was Sunday, and he had spent the morning finishing a draft of his paper on Harlem Renaissance iconography for his Critical Studies in the Visual Arts class. The rest of the day would be spent getting ready for his exhibit.

The exhibit wasn't for school, but at least two of his professors were coming, including his prospectus advisor, who would be giving him ideas for his prospectus and final exhibition based on this showing. Some pieces that weren't sold might even go into his final exhibition.

At the same time, he was hoping that the showing would give him some exposure. To that end, he'd taken out ads in three papers, two magazines and two theater programs. He'd also made and copied flyers that he was going to start putting up today, and he'd even had postcards printed that he'd been giving out here and there for a few weeks.

He spent the early part of the afternoon selecting pieces and building bases, but he needed more supplies, so he wrapped up what he was doing and changed to go out. He brought postcards and flyers with him and went to pick up his little brother.

"Where are we off to?" Lawrence asked.

"A little bit of everywhere. But the first stop is the fabric store."

"Fabric?"

"I need material and batting for backdrops."

"Okay. I can help with that. What next?"

"Next," Darien said, "is the hardware store for heavy-gauge wire and picture hangers, platforms of some kind, some extra lighting."

"Have you started working on the location as yet?"

"No, that comes at the end—next week. It'll take at least two days to install the whole thing, assuming I can get some help."

Lawrence looked out the window as if occupied. Darien knuckled his head and then started to pull it down for more.

"All right," Lawrence said. "I'll help."

"I'm borrowing the van, the ladder and a couple of moving dollies from the Heritage Center. We should be able to make out. I'll be forever grateful."

"I wouldn't leave you stranded."

Darien didn't take too long in the fabric store, despite his brother's meandering. Lawrence found a piece of hot-pink fabric with sequins and held it up against his chest.

"I can see Safire in this," he said. "How are things with her? You know she came and spoke to us at the gala."

Darien grimaced and nodded. "No sequins. I mostly need basic colors—black, white, beige, fire-engine red, sky blue, ocean cobalt, grass green. Oh, and some African prints."

"I'd have guessed that," Lawrence said. "But you didn't answer my question."

"Not well. Now, focus."

"Want to talk to baby brother about it?"

Darien looked at his brother. "Not now, but thank you. Is there anything you need to tell your big brother about? Any*one?*"

Lawrence exhaled and hung his head down. "No, not right now. I guess I wanted to live vicariously through you for a little bit."

"We'll have to change that," Darien said. "But for now—" he tapped a bolt of fabric "—come on. We have a dozen stops to make."

Lawrence fluffed a shaggy orange fabric, and Darien shook his head. He wasn't going to get very far if he waited on his little brother to make selections. He finally started handing Lawrence the bolts that he wanted and had Lawrence take them to the counter for cutting. He saved time that way, and Lawrence didn't need to concentrate when his mind was elsewhere.

They made quick work of the hardware store, and then they started dropping off postcards and flyers. The largest stack of postcards went into the mailbox outside the post office. He'd gotten permission to send them out to the mailing list for the Heritage Center, and others were going to arts organizations all over the city, with packets going to some of the museums.

The flyers were going to specific businesses in the area that allowed postings, like cafés and restaurants. This meant a bunch of little stops, some with permission inquiries. They did what they could and stopped for dinner at seven. Then Darien dropped his brother off at his apartment with a thankful hug and headed home.

It had already been a full day, but Darien had a full night ahead of him. He had some small tables from the hardware store to put together. He also had some pieces he was still working on and several he wanted to seal. Others needed holes or metal pieces for hanging. Some he just needed to make decisions about.

When all that was done, he started working again on the Safire piece. It wasn't going in his art show, but it was almost finished, and he wanted it completely done. Coincidentally, this is what he was doing when the phone rang.

It was Safire, and Safire wasn't happy. In fact, even the way she said hello made it sound as if she wanted to pick a fight.

"Safire? Is anything wrong?"

"In fact, yes. I want to know why you disappeared in the bookstore, sneaking off behind my back. I couldn't let you have it at the fund-raiser, but now you better have a pretty good explanation."

Darien sighed. "So you've called. Did it take you this long to miss me?" He could almost feel Safire rearing up to strike. "Did I hit a nerve?"

"You can miss my black—"

"Let's not be vulgar," Darien cut in.

"You have no idea what I can be. And I won't be dismissed either."

Darien put down his chisel and took off his goggles. "You want to have it out, Safire? Let's have it out."

"Why did you leave?" she said.

"I was not going to stand around and argue with you in the bookstore. As touching as your jealousy was, I've never been the one giving you a reason to be jealous."

"Next time, be a man and take your leave. And I was not jealous, only surprised by how quickly Mr. Let's-Go-Slow filled my shoes."

Darien tried to be level, yet this woman disturbed his calm so easily. "As I said, it wasn't like that. I was not encouraging the attention."

"You didn't seem to be running her off, either."

"So you are jealous," Darien said. "I guess this is a nice change. But for the record, you're the one who doesn't want to commit. I'm the one who's not interested in the casual."

"Here you go again with that nonsense. Casual is your code for loose, and that's not what I offered," Safire said, seething. "That's your hang-up from being burned before."

"Hold up," Darien said, ready to tell this woman what was what. "You think you had my number the first day we met, but I've seen a few things about you, too. You know what I think? I think that losing your parents made you afraid you'll lose anyone you get too close to. So you play the field, and you play it light. But all that means is that nobody stands a chance." In the brief pause that followed, Darien quieted down. "But you did miss me, didn't you?"

"The world doesn't revolve around you, Darien James."

"Or—"

Safire hung up, cutting him off. Darien let out a guttural roar and banged down the phone. This woman made him psycho, but she was all he wanted. Only Safire would call him, missing him, actually, and proceed by picking a fight. Only she would call him, still jealous, mind you, and go on to test his cool.

And he had stepped right into it and gone where he didn't intend. He didn't mean to bring up the whole question of the casual again. In fact, he'd meant a casual relationship, not casual sex. He didn't think their intimacy was casual to her. Or did he?

Darien was still in his studio, and he walked around his Safire piece. The contradictions she embodied could confuse even a thoughtful man.

He thought about what his brother had said about waiting, not pushing. He'd messed that up—again. He wanted her to take him and their relationship seriously. He hadn't advanced that cause—at all.

He also thought about Safire, who she was and what his piece was turning out to be. He looked at it, really looked. In some ways, Safire was turning out to be an amalgamation of every woman he'd ever known. Mostly, however, she was turning out be her own unique, evolving creation.

Darien sat down at his table, holding his gaze on the Safire piece. For the first time it made him think of the other women he'd known—the ones who'd burned him. He was carrying baggage, and it did shade his perspective on Safire. It did make him misread her or read into her, especially at first. Was he still doing that? Was that why he'd jumped at the first chance to keep pushing? Deep down, his experiences in the past made him assume that she wouldn't commit. Darien swallowed this dawning self-knowledge like a bitter cube of ice.

And what now? He'd been wondering how much time she needed. Now she probably needed years. Darien stood and put on his goggles and picked up his chisel. He didn't want to wait years, not even one, and he was going to get this piece done. One way or another, he was going to capture Safire.

Chapter 19

Safire knocked on Mr. Benson's door. "Here is the research for the Coles case," she said.

"Thank you," he replied and looked at his watch. "Hey, it's after six. Get out of here before I find something else for you to do."

"I'm almost finished packing up already."

Mr. Benson laughed. "I'll be right behind you."

Safire returned to the law library, finished shelving the last of the books she'd been using and grabbed her blazer from the back of the chair.

It was a Friday night, and she had decided to go to happy hour at Jake's. It had been a long week, and she wanted a little recreation. Unfortunately, she found herself at a table with hot wings and a virgin strawberry daiquiri, and she couldn't help thinking of the first day she'd met Darien James.

It had been almost a week since she'd called him to let him have it about ditching her in the bookstore. That hadn't gone as planned; in fact, she hadn't really had a plan. She wasn't sure what she expected, but an apology would have been good. Instead, she got an argument.

But the truth was that she did miss Darien. She had probably even come here because she missed him. She knew that the memory of him was waiting here for her. She'd missed him in Houston. She'd missed him when she got back. Why hadn't she just said so? He might have had an idea about that, about why it was so hard for her to get close to people and stay close. Even Angelina had guessed that she was sabotaging things because…because she wanted it to be serious.

Her own jealousy showed her how deep the river of her feelings ran. She didn't want to keep hurting, and Darien was the salve for her turmoil. Anger helped her to avoid the sting, but it didn't make the misery go away. Her feelings for him had been growing like roots all along, but she couldn't say that to him when she hadn't been ready to admit it to herself. He'd been right about practically everything. Now she could lose this man because of her own misdirected rage. She could lose him over the silence she had pledged to break. Maybe she already had.

Safire pulled out her phone and called Darien's number. She didn't know what she was going to say, only that she wanted to see him, only that it was time for the truth.

She needn't have worried. He wasn't in. Oh, yeah, this was one of his days at the Heritage Center. She didn't get him, but his answering machine had changed. He was on it talking about the exhibit he had coming up. He'd mentioned that. The opening was next Saturday night.

Safire called back and took down the information. Before she knew what she was thinking, she was already planning to surprise him that night at his show. She also had a favor to call in from her soon-to-be brother-in-law, so she could do a little more than show up; she could help get the word out.

She was excited to do something for the effort. In fact, she was excited that she'd be seeing Darien again and anxious to say what there was to be said. There would be no turning back this time, not on account of her. But regardless of what happened to them, Safire had seen Darien's art, and it was worth supporting.

Safire checked her watch and decided to visit the gallery where the opening was taking place. She had a few things to put in motion and just enough time to do them.

After a few stops and a few calls and a visit to her sister, where she had a powwow about the wedding plans and checked on her little brother, Safire headed home. She was tired, and she wouldn't be seeing Darien until next weekend. She could have gone out with her girls, but she wasn't in the mood. She called Camilla and made plans to meet with her friends for dinner during the week.

By the time she changed for bed, it was after eleven o'clock, and within minutes, Safire was fast asleep.

She woke up to the ringing of her phone.

She checked the clock, and it was already nine. She picked up the receiver and answered the call.

"Hello, Safire."

It was Darien. Safire sat up, wondering what had made him call her. Had he found out that she'd gone to the gallery and was snooping around?

"I've wanted to talk to you," Darien said, "not argue but talk."

"I called you yesterday," Safire admitted.

"I know. I saw your number on my machine."

Safire pushed the covers off and put her feet on the floor. "I didn't call to argue. I…I thought we should talk, too."

"I have my Saturday classes at the Heritage Center, but maybe we can have dinner tonight."

"Okay."

"I'll pick you up at seven."

"I'll be ready."

Safire was kept busy during the day, but that evening she turned her attention to the thoughts that has been threatening to surface all day. She was seeing Darien again, and this time she didn't want to argue. It was time to tell him the truth.

Safire changed into a short, knit teal dress. It had a belt that went around the waist and crossed over her chest to form the shoulders, and she liked the way it hugged her body. Darien picked her up at seven wearing his denims with a white shirt and a bright purple vest. They hugged briefly in a cordial way, but it was clear that they hadn't broken the ice as yet. They were saving the heavy stuff for later—after dinner.

They went to a quiet seafood restaurant, where they ordered and ate. It wasn't until after dessert that they really began to talk.

"Safire," Darien said, "I want to make things work between us. Or at least give them a chance to work. I haven't done that."

His tone was sincere, and Safire felt her heart surge and any remaining resistance fall away.

"My exhibit opens next weekend," he said, "and I can't imagine you not being there. I can't imagine you not seeing how much you've been an inspiration in my art since I've known you. I—"

"I want to say something, too," Safire said. "You asked me if I missed you, and I guess I never answered. I have missed you. I do miss you. And it's never been just physical with you for me."

"I'm sorry I brought that up again on the phone," Darien said, taking her hands. "I think our hang-ups work against each other."

"What?" she asked.

"Because I've been burned," Darien said, "part of me figures that nobody wants to commit. So I pushed when I shouldn't—"

"And because I've lost people I love," Safire said, "part

of me figures that maybe I'll lose anyone I love, so I push people away or sabotage things when—"

"When things get too serious."

Safire's eyes had become moist as she spoke. She didn't know why, only that this man had always been a haven for her tears.

Darien scooted over next to Safire in their booth and drew her into his arms.

"If you promise not to sabotage," he said against her ear, "I'll promise not to push."

Her eyes were still wet, but Safire smiled and wrapped her arms around Darien's shoulders.

"It's a deal," she said, holding on tight.

When she let his shoulders loose, Darien pulled back just enough to find Safire's lips with his own. They remained locked to one another until their waitress cleared her throat, depositing the check on the table.

Darien paid the bill, and they walked to his car.

"Where to now?" Darien asked.

Safire put herself in Darien's embrace and tangled her arms around his neck. She kissed him deeply and then rested her forehead along his cheek.

"Take me home with you tonight," she said.

"Are you sure?" Darien asked.

She nodded, and he pressed her hard against his chest.

"I've missed you, too, Safire," he said. "I've missed you so much."

Safire parked her car and checked her face. It was the opening night of Darien's exhibition, and although he knew she was coming, he didn't know that she had invited her family and friends and their friends.

Safire had wanted to wear something special for tonight. She settled on an orchid gown made of woven satin. The skirt of the dress was short and had rhinestones emblazoning the bottom hem and covering the bust. It also had an empire waist, and the bodice was low cut in front and in back. It had spaghetti straps and showed off all of her curves.

She had on three-inch heels and had a matching purse, and she also wore a large silver cuff bracelet and a thin silver necklace. Her long, freshly done curls hung down her back, and she'd done up her face and painted her nails. Now she walked toward Darien's exhibit with a bouquet of roses in her hands.

The gallery had been operating all day, but the official opening was from six to ten. The Elizabeth Hellard Fine Art Gallery was in the heart of the Wynwood Art District in Miami. It sometimes represented emerging artists and had apparently seen what Safire had seen in Darien's work. They'd offered him a solo exhibit in what was actually a large exhibition space.

It was six-thirty when Safire got there. She wanted to be early because she knew it would be busy later. She found Darien talking to the gallery owner at the reception area just inside. He had on a blue suit and a matching kente cloth tie with a white shirt, and when he saw her, a broad smile emerged from his face. He stepped toward her, and she held out the flowers.

"Thank you," he said, taking them from her.

"Let me go find a vase," said the owner.

Before she got back, Darien took out one of the roses and handed it to Safire.

"You look exquisite," he said and then kissed her.

Safire smiled and smelled the rose. Darien laid the bouquet on the table next to the champagne glasses and took Safire's hand.

"You're early, so it's pretty quiet. Do you want a tour?"

"I was hoping for one."

"We've partitioned the space into four rooms. This is the first one, my favorite."

A plaque indicated that the room had two themes, "The People Could Fly" and "The Ibo Landing Story," both based on African-American folk narratives about slaves flying or walking on the water back to Africa. Sky-blue fabric and batting covered the ceiling, and wood carvings of black people flying east were suspended from the ceiling, some as low down as eye level. The closer ones were life-size, and the ones farther up were smaller, giving the impression of altitude.

"The way you capture their movement is amazing," Safire said. "I feel like I'm in the clouds with them."

"Excellent," Darien said. "That was my goal."

Farther into the room, shiny cobalt-blue fabric covered the floor—an ocean—and here the wooden figures were walking toward the east—slaves, nineteenth- and twentieth-century people, modern people. The impression of distance was given by making the farther ones smaller. Safire was astonished. The installation was awe inspiring.

The next room was smaller and had a plaque reading, The Trickster Across Cultures. Here the figures were mounted on pedestals or tables with fabric backdrops in black velvet, white cotton and African prints. It was impossible to take in all of them. Safire walked around the room, looking at individual pieces. One was of an old black man with two faces pointing off in opposite directions like the god Janus. One was of Anansi the spider from Ashanti lore; the spider had a man's head. One was of three black women whose gowns billowed over a cliff—sirens, she presumed. There were many others, and they were all so detailed, so realistic.

The next room was "Family Routes" and amid a host of Africa family tree statues of all sizes and configurations were carvings of people—all kinds—on backdrops of grass-green fabric that also covered the floor. One walked through the room as if on a path through the park, and two of the life-size carvings were of people on park benches with space for actual people to sit. This room also had sketches and paintings.

The last room was "The Growing Tree," and it was a collection of just about everything. Wood carvings and reliefs were on beige-fabric backdrops, and ceramic pieces were on bright red backdrops. There were sketches and paintings, as well as lamps, bowls, partitions, figures—too many things of too many different kinds to name.

"What is the theme here?" Safire asked, turning to Darien.

He was staring at her, and instead of answering her question, he pulled her into his arms and kissed her.

"What was that for?" Safire asked after their kiss had ended.

"I don't know," Darien said. "I'm just glad you're here. You're more beautiful than anything I could ever create."

Safire was touched by his earnestness and reached up to cup his cheek. "These are wonderful, so that's really saying something."

As they were about to kiss again, a couple walked in. Safire smiled and turned back to the room. Darien held her from behind, put his chin on her shoulder and looked with her.

"Yes, the theme," he said. "This room doesn't have one. It's miscellaneous—one to grow on."

It was after seven, and people had started arriving, so the owner called Darien to come greet guests. Darien took Safire's hand and obeyed, and he kept her hand all night, except when she pulled away to hug someone or talk to someone, as when her family came—Angelina, Jeremy, Philly and Alex. Her friends had also started arriving, as well as people from Benson and Hines. People also came from Jeremy's job—doctors and nurses—and from Angelina's—professors and staff. And Jeremy's friends also came, including ones Safire had met.

"You asked all those people to come, didn't you?"

Safire smiled.

People also came because of Darien's efforts—students and parents from the Heritage Center, people from its mailing list, people from some of the places he'd sent flyers to, people from some of the places where he'd put posters up, people interested by his ads in the papers and magazines, his brother and mother, his classmates, his teachers, his friends. His mother had even gotten people from her church to come.

Sold signs started going up next to the title plates for various pieces. For Darien, it wasn't about the money but about the start of his reputation as an artist. The owner kept busy talking up the pieces and the emerging artist, but she gave Darien the thumbs-up sign whenever a piece was sold. Once, she did it when Jeremy was standing next to her. The two men nodded at each other, and Darien turned to Safire.

"You made him do that, didn't you?"

Safire laughed. "I don't have to make anyone get your art, honey. It's good."

They hugged and continued mingling.

Two of Darien's teachers came by at one point, and Darien introduced Safire.

"You have a real artist here," one said to her. Then she turned to Darien. "You have an A for Figure Sculpture. Come get your final projects so that you can put them in the exhibit."

The other shook Safire's free hand and then nodded to Darien. "You can also expect an A for your final exhibition. This should have been it. Is this your first real exhibit?"

"Yes, sir, it is."

"Come see me next term to talk more about the prospectus."

"I will. Thank you," Darien said.

Darien turned to her and kissed the hand he was holding. "I have to keep you with me always," he said. "You're my talisman."

Mr. Johnson came by and hugged them both. And Safire got to see Lawrence and Mrs. James again. Her family also came to hug Darien, and some of her friends met him, as well. Camilla gave her a sly wink and held her hand up like a phone, indicating that they would be talking. All the while, Darien kept her hand in his.

Safire stayed until it was time to close. After Darien spoke to the owner, he walked her to her car, and they went to a late supper. Then he took her home to his apartment. With everything out in the open between them, they were free to be with one another again, and Safire drew Darien into the bedroom.

The wall between them had broken apart at the restaurant, and their new bond had expanded at the gallery. Suddenly, they had nothing left to hide. Suddenly, their lives were intertwined.

Chapter 20

Safire had been busy with Angelina all morning. It was her sister's wedding day, and she wanted it to bc perfect. She crossed the vestibule entry of the church as Darien stepped inside wearing a black suit with a red tie. He was her date, so his tie matched her red bridesmaid dress. There were four bridesmaids, and they all wore gowns made of that same bright red chiffon, each tailored to the style of the wearer.

Safire's was sleeveless and backless, and the top half fit her like the bustier that she wore underneath it. The bottom half was a short, uneven hem skirt that fluttered about her mid-to-upper thighs. All the bridesmaids wore silver slippers. Safire's were three-inch strappy heels. Her hair was done up on top of her head, and long silver earrings dangled from her ears, matching her silver necklace and silver hibiscus bracelet.

While the bride carried a bouquet of white French roses, all of the bridesmaids carried red anemones, including Safire, the maid of honor. She dipped at her knees in a curtsy when she saw Darien. She smiled at him like a Cheshire cat, and waved on the sly from her hip. Without a word, she kissed him briefly and then ran off to see about her sister.

Darien sucked in his breath at the sight of Safire and

didn't let it out until she had disappeared. Red was a fitting color for her, and that mixture of innocence and fire was captured in her dress and her curtsy, her smile and her manner. He had stood dumbfounded, unable to say a word as she whisked by, stopping only to get her lipstick on his lips.

Now Darien followed the procession of visitors into the nave of the church and took a seat on the second row with others similarly attired. His mother and brother had come in earlier and were seated farther back in the audience.

It was three days after Christmas, which Safire and Darien had spent together—first at his mother's house with his family and then at her sister's house with her family and soon-to-be in-laws. Darien recognized the best man, Alistair, and the other groomsmen, including Alex, from the rehearsal dinner the previous night. There was Eddy, the groom's brother, and Myron and Rudy, the groom's friends. Alistair's partner, Reggie, sat next to Darien.

The week before, Darien's exhibit had closed, having done remarkably well, and the same week, Safire had given her sister's bachelorette party, scandalizing Angelina with her sexy gift, as expected. Now Safire lined up with Michelle, one of Jeremy's best friends, and two friends of her sister. Jeremy's mother was in the audience, but his father was giving the bride away. The ring bearers were Phillip and Tyler, and they were all ready. The violins stopped playing and the organ sounded the first chord, and it began, Safire not far behind Angelina.

As handsome as the groom was and as radiant as the bride was, Safire and Darien spent the ceremony looking at each other and smiling. Darien gazed at Safire over the two bouquets of flowers she was holding—one red, one white—and saw his Safire piece in motion and color. Mostly, though, he looked at her smiling at him and thought about the possibility of their future together.

Safire looked at her hottie and thought about the sweetness and passion of the night before, after the rehearsal dinner. She savored his gorgeous smile and dreamed about what a wedding with him would look and feel like—being filled with love for an amazing man, having his expression fixed on her with that eternal adoration. Could she have a love like that? Could she give it? She thought that maybe with this man she could.

Safire didn't get to talk to Darien until after the ceremony and the pictures and the toasts, when they were dancing together at the reception.

Held in his arms on the floor of the banquet hall, Safire felt as if it was her wedding, and holding her in his arms, Darien felt like African royalty.

"What are you smiling at?" Safire asked.

"Being with you," Darien replied, and kissed her.

"We have to get as much of it now as we can because I'll be watching my baby brother for the next two weeks. I won't get to see you every day."

"We don't see each other every day now, but I'm going to miss you," Darien said, holding Safire closer. "You know, I can help watch your brother with you, if that's okay with your family."

"You better count on it," she said. "And they'll be moving as well, so you get to help with that, too."

Darien glanced at the bride and groom. "Where will the couple be going on their honeymoon?"

"They met on a cruise," Safire said, "so they're going on a cruise at the same time. That's why they got married right after Christmas."

"That's really beautiful," he said. "Where should we go on ours?"

Safire smiled. She liked that Darien would think of them as having a honeymoon together. "Let's see. We met at the Law Offices of Benson and Hines."

They both chuckled, and Darien dipped Safire in their

dance. "Don't be funny," he said. "How about Palm Beach? That was our first vacation together, even though we argued."

Safire brought her arm from Darien's neck and touched his face. "I don't ever want to fight with you again."

A shudder moved through Darien's body, and he was filled with tenderness for this woman. He kissed her briefly because that was all he could do to show what had just filled him inside.

"Thank you," Safire said.

"You never have to thank me for a kiss," Darien said softly.

Heat started building up in Safire. Darien's soft voice always did that to her. She had to shake her head to clear it.

"Palm Beach has sentimental value," Safire said wistfully.

"That's what I was thinking," Darien said and held her.

Darien caught Safire by the waist before she could sit down and kissed her ear. This made her smile. She poked his hard chest with her finger and turned to him for a kiss on the lips, which he was more than happy to give.

Safire slid into the chair at Darien's dining table and began eating her eggs and toast. Darien got his cereal and brought juice for both of them and sat next to her. He had on fresh gray sweatpants and a long-sleeved, gray waffle-weave pullover. Safire had on what she wore about the house—blue leggings and a blue racer-back tank top with one-inch sandals. She had just showered, and her hair was pulled back in a ponytail.

"You know," Darien said, "you can leave some things here so that you don't have to pack an overnight bag all the time."

"I might," Safire said. "And you can do the same thing when you're over by me."

"Yes, but we spend more time here."

"I know," she said. "Your place is homey, and mine has a roommate."

Darien smiled and pulled one of Safire's hands to his mouth to kiss it. "Either one is fine with me," he said.

Safire stopped eating and leaned toward Darien. "I have news."

"Tell me."

"I've decided about going back to school next year. I got into both of the programs that I applied to, and I plan to do the Master's of Science in Curriculum and Instruction in English Education. Then I plan to go to law school and focus on children's issues and education. I plan to teach and practice law—together."

"That's great," Darien said. "You've decided."

"It'll take a little while before I'm finished, but—"

"But all that matters is what you love."

"I love both."

Darien scooted his chair closer to Safire and pulled her into a hug. Safire had been holding her breath, unsure of how her revelation would be taken. She relaxed into Darien's embrace and sighed, grateful to have it received this way. It made her surer of her herself and what she hoped to do.

Darien sat back. "I've been thinking about some things, as well," he said.

"Like what?" Safire asked. She wanted to give Darien the support he had just shown her, so she turned to him.

"I plan to put some of my pieces online whenever I can get a website together."

"Uh-huh. That's a great idea."

"It's not for the money. I have that. It's because I need to know I can get established as an artist, develop a reputation, a following. If I can do that, then I can open a real shop or gallery somewhere. I've already started mapping out the website," Darien said. "After I finish my MFA, I'm going to start as an ebusiness—both original pieces and some made-to-order pieces, like the lamps. I'd still be working at the Heritage Center and maybe teaching or—"

"That sounds wonderful. Before long, you'll have a gallery of your own—maybe something in the Wynwood Art District. That would be excellent."

"Once I get going, I plan to advertise. If I can keep having showings and gaining exposure, it can work—"

Safire got out of her chair and plopped down on Darien's lap, throwing her arms around his neck. "I've seen your art," she said. "It's definitely going to work."

Darien felt blessed by Safire's confidence. "You know," he said, "I love having you to dream with."

Safire pulled her legs up on Darien's lap, and he pulled her against him, kissing her.

"Are you finished eating?" he asked.

Safire nodded.

"There's something I want to show you."

"What?"

Darien lifted Safire and set them both on the floor standing. "You have to see it," he said.

"Okay," she said. Safire was intrigued and let herself be guided into Darien's bedroom workshop.

The shelves were barer than before, but near the center of the room, a sheet covered…something.

Darien didn't know what Safire would think of his creation, but he took a breath and pulled the sheet from over it. It was the Safire piece, finally fully finished.

The center of the piece was a life-size figure of Safire, and the large surrounding base held smaller figures and relief. It was primarily carved wood, but there was some of everything contributing to the finished sculpture—metal pieces, wood burning, mosaic work, ceramic work, stained glass. Some sections were overlaid with gold foil. Some were painted. Some had inlay work. Some were covered with glass. Various colors of stain were used to give variety to the wood.

"Come," Darien said. "You have to see it from here—" he drew her to one side "—and here." He drew her to the other side "—and here." He drew her to the front.

"Oh, my God," Safire said. "That's incredible."

Darien stepped back as Safire resumed the first station, then the second, then the third. From one side she seemed sweet and innocent. This was because her expression was serene and her hand was open, palm upward, holding a dove. From the other side she seemed sexy and naughty. This was because this side of her mouth curved up slightly in a smile, puckering her cheek, and because her hand on this side gripped her skirt and lifted it up just a bit. From the front, she simply seemed whole—like herself.

"How did you do that?" she asked.

Darien was happy that Safire had gotten what he'd tried to do. "It's called *Sweet Seductress.* I hope it works. I tried to capture something of your spirit—soft and sassy, girl and woman."

Safire bent down and started circling the figure, looking at the base. Darien watched her. The base stretched as wide as the figure was high, and carved into it were family trees, people, relief figures, abstracts—all of this surrounding the central figure, as if she was the guiding angel. Instead of a simple figure, it was an entire narrative, telling the whole African-American story from slavery through the presidency.

"Look at all of this," Safire said, rounding the figure. "It's so detailed. It's unbelievable."

"I hope you like it. The base took longer than the central figure, but both were difficult to capture."

"I love it," she said. "It's like looking in a mirror and into history."

Safire came to stand in front of the figure, and Darien wrapped his arms around her, looking at it with her, trying to see what she saw. Safire saw that Darien had understood something of the inside of her, that he had seen her and accepted her. She covered his hands with her own and simply gazed at the piece, thinking of all the time he must have put into it. He must have been working on it when they were arguing and when they were apart.

Darien saw Safire admiring the piece and was satisfied down to the bone. All the work had been worth it if she liked it. No one else mattered.

Darien closed his eyes and smelled Safire's freshly bathed neck. Although Safire had been the one to initiate their physical relationship, Darien had never been able to resist her, and now that he knew her enough to trust her, he didn't have to. Her neck had the sultry aroma of her perfume on it, and Darien kissed it.

Safire felt a tingle radiate from Darien's kiss across her back and down her spine. Then she felt one of his hands move from her waist to her breasts—first one and then the other. Her nipples constricted, and flames shot into her loins.

Darien felt Safire's hips stir and heard her intake of breath, and his body was lit on fire. His pulse raced and his manhood began to throb. He moved his other hand from Safire's waist and ran it up and down her outer thighs and then up her inner thigh until he found the center of her body and began stroking her there.

Safire murmured, and her hips began to toil in circles, bringing her both to Darien's hand and to the sweet swelling behind her. Her sex started to pulse, and she felt moisture soak through her underwear. With his mouth moving across her shoulders, Darien's hands ravished her until she was panting, until she felt as if she was flying and drowning and singing all at once. His hands filled her with a need so acute that it ached. She couldn't calm her breathing.

Darien's body was responding to each signal made by Safire. Every whimper made him jerk. Every gyration made him ready. The rotating pressure of her rump against his groin made him thicken and quicken and leap. When he couldn't stand any more, he stepped back from her. She turned to him, hungry for his lips, and wrapped her arms around his neck. He lifted her against his body, and she moaned. Then he lifted her off the ground and carried her to his room.

Once inside, he laid her on the bed and began taking off her clothes. His mouth found her breasts as he freed them from her tank top and bra, and the way her back arched upward, bringing her to meet his lips, created a succulent image in his mind. Then Safire felt him pull down the waist of her leggings, his lips traveling over her belly to the delicate bud below. She winced as he covered her, his mouth wreaking sweet havoc on her senses, filling her with need.

Darien leaned up and stepped back when Safire tried to take hold of him. But he stopped only long enough to pull her sandals from her feet, tear the clothes off his body and rifle through one of his drawers. He came back to her wearing a condom. Safire smiled and spread her body for him to possess, wanting to belong to this man.

And he wanted her to be his. He covered her and slipped his thighs between her legs. He moved up her body until he was poised at her gate, where he knew she loved to be teased. Safire filled with yearning and began to squirm against the sweet torture, wanting fuller contact.

In the middle of this, Darien laughed.

Safire swatted at him, but she was smiling.

"You like tormenting me this way, don't you?" she asked.

"I love tormenting you this way," he replied. "It turns me on infinitely. Can't you feel how ready I am?"

"Yes," Safire said, and her eyes fluttered closed. "Make love to me."

"Actually," Darien said, "there's something you should know."

Safire opened her eyes. Darien raised himself up on his elbows, and he looked at Safire, his muse. "I love you, Safire. I love you so much. I've loved you a long time, but I didn't want to say anything and chase you away. You don't have to say anything. I just need you to know."

Tears came to Safire's eyes. There was a time when she would have been frightened away by hearing that, but not now. She put one of her hands to Darien's cheek. "I love you, too," Safire said. "I love you, too."

Darien was elated. A wide smile cut across his face. He leaned down and kissed Safire, first lovingly, then passionately. Then he moved inside her, filling her.

Safire tilted her hips to meet Darien's thrust and wrapped her legs around him, pulling him farther inside. He had teased her until she was slick and ready. Now her body clamped on to his as they began to move together—love and passion blurring into one as their bodies merged.

Safire's breasts grazed against Darien's chest, and he reached a hand between them to play with her breasts and her blossom. Safire's torso twisted in delight, and a heavy pulse started to throb inside her. Darien felt himself gripped in the tight embrace of Safire's desire and watched as she moved against his palm and fingertips. The sight of her rapture spurred his yearning, and his pace quickened.

Safire called Darien's name as her sex contracted around his leaping member and exploded into convulsions that shook her body. Darien answered yes as his body became rigid and started to buck in short, hard jerks. He felt the waves of Safire's climax encase him as he poured out his love.

Darien cupped both sides of Safire's head and kissed

her. His kiss was deep but gentle, claiming and loving this woman. And Safire returned it, drinking in Darien's soft, thick chocolate lips and returning his claim and his love.

Darien moved from above Safire and settled next to her, wrapping his arms around her as she spooned against him, her back to his chest. Safire put her arms over the ones at her waist and wove her fingers into Darien's.

For no apparent reason, Safire started to chuckle.

Darien tickled her hips. "Why are you laughing?"

"At one point, I thought that maybe you didn't like sexual intimacy as much as I do."

Darien laughed. As much as this woman had turned him on from the very beginning, she had to be kidding.

"That's not true."

Safire smiled. "I know."

Darien ran his fingers over Safire's arms. "Is it true that you love me? Are you in love with me?"

Although it had started as one of her typical momentary pursuits, Safire had become captivated by this man. And now he finally knew. She nodded and found the hands that were rubbing her arms.

"Then marry me, Safire," Darien said. "I love you, too."

"What?"

"Marry me."

Safire turned around to look into Darien's face. It held such devotion, such love, such anticipation that it arrested her.

"Yes," she said, tears filling her eyes. "I love you, and I'll marry you."

Darien's heart lit up like fireworks, and his face fanned out into a wide-open grin. Safire swiped at her tears, smiling through the streaks on her face.

"I want a wooden ring," she said.

"Hell, no," Darien replied. "I mean, I'll make you a

wooden ring, but our engagement and wedding rings have to be gold."

"Why?"

"Because you're precious," Darien said and kissed her eyelid, "and because my mother and brother would kill me if I gave you a wooden wedding ring."

Safire laughed and stroked the ridges along Darien's chest.

"You'll be stuck with me," she said.

"I want to be stuck with you," he responded, bringing her face to his.

Safire kissed Darien's lips. "I want to be stuck with you, too."

Their kisses turned from soft to hard. A heat was building between them again. Darien rolled onto his back, bringing Safire with him. She straddled his thighs and sat up. Then she watched as he reached into his nightstand, removed the old condom and put on a fresh one.

Darien saw Safire's Cheshire cat grin spread over her face, and she leaned down, purring. Darien laughed. Then he toppled Safire over and covered her body with his own.

Their lips met, and their laughter turned to murmurs. Darien reached between them and touched his fragile flower. Safire arched, feeling a flame bloom throughout her body. She put her hands to Darien's chest and closed her fingers around his nipples. Darien's body leaped at Safire's command, filling with hunger.

"I love you," Darien said.

"I love you, too," Safire replied.

Darien entered his sweet seductress, and Safire clung to her hot Adonis.

This was the start of their union.

* * * * *